Allison stiffened at the whisper-light brush of fingers against her nape.

Startled, she spun to confront whomever had touched her, but found no one. She stood at the edge of the group and though the room was crowded, no one was within arm's reach.

How odd. Puzzled, she turned back to the lecturer.

Within moments, she felt the same brush against her nape. Frowning, she glanced over her shoulder. But again, no one stood close enough to have touched her.

Her gaze swept the crowd and she went perfectly still.

Across the packed ballroom, a man leaned against a marble pillar, watching her.

Allison felt his intent black gaze as surely as if he'd reached out, slipped his arm around her waist and pulled her body against his.

He is what I felt, she thought, dazed.

Dear Reader,

As you take a break from raking those autumn leaves, you'll want to check out our latest Silhouette Special Edition novels! This month, we're thrilled to feature Stella Bagwell's *Should Have Been Her Child* (#1570), the first book in her new miniseries, MEN OF THE WEST. Stella writes that this series is full of "rough, tough cowboys, the strong bond of sibling love and the wide-open skies of the west. Mix those elements with a dash of intrigue, mayhem and a whole lot of romance and you get the Ketchum family!" And we can't wait to read their stories!

Next, Christine Rimmer brings us *The Marriage Medallion* (#1567), the third book in her VIKING BRIDES series, which is all about matrimonial destiny and solving secrets of the past. In Jodi O'Donnell's *The Rancher's Daughter* (#1568), part of popular series MONTANA MAVERICKS: THE KINGSLEYS, two unlikely soul mates are trapped in a cave…and find a way to stay warm. *Practice Makes Pregnant* (#1569) by Lois Faye Dyer, the fourth book in the MANHATTAN MULTIPLES series, tells the story of a night of passion and a very unexpected development between a handsome attorney and a bashful assistant. Will their marriage of convenience turn to everlasting love?

Patricia Kay will hook readers into an intricate family dynamic and heart-thumping romance in *Secrets of a Small Town* (#1571). And Karen Sandler's *Counting on a Cowboy* (#1572) is an engaging tale about a good-hearted teacher who finds love with a rancher and his young daughter. You won't want to miss this touching story!

Stay warm in this crisp weather with six complex and satisfying romances. And be sure to return next month for more emotional storytelling from Silhouette Special Edition!

Happy reading!

Gail Chasan
Senior Editor

Please address questions and book requests to:
Silhouette Reader Service
U.S.: 3010 Walden Ave., P.O. Box 1325, Buffalo, NY 14269
Canadian: P.O. Box 609, Fort Erie, Ont. L2A 5X3

Practice Makes Pregnant

LOIS FAYE DYER

Silhouette

SPECIAL EDITION™

Published by Silhouette Books

America's Publisher of Contemporary Romance

Special thanks and acknowledgment are given to
Lois Faye Dyer for her contribution to the
MANHATTAN MULTIPLES series.

For Rose Marie Lunny-Harris,
in memory of her mother,
Hazel Lunny.

 SILHOUETTE BOOKS

ISBN 0-373-24569-6

PRACTICE MAKES PREGNANT

Books by Lois Faye Dyer

Silhouette Special Edition

Lonesome Cowboy #1038
He's Got His Daddy's Eyes #1129
The Cowboy Takes a Wife #1198
The Only Cowboy for Caitlin #1253
Cattleman's Courtship #1306
Cattleman's Bride-To-Be #1457
Practice Makes Pregnant #1569

LOIS FAYE DYER

lives on Washington State's beautiful Puget Sound with her husband, their yellow Lab, Maggie Mae, and two eccentric cats. She loves to hear from readers and you can write to her c/o Paperbacks Plus, 1618 Bay Street, Port Orchard, WA 98366.

MANHATTAN MULTIPLES

So much excitement happening at once!

The doors of Manhattan Multiples might shut down. The mayor and Eloise Vale once had a thing. Someone on the staff is pregnant and is keeping it a secret. Romance and drama—and so many babies in the big city!

Jorge Perez—Manhattan's hottest assistant district attorney, determined to fight for justice, too busy for love. At a social function, Jorge sees a shy beauty and knows he *has* to talk to her. He crosses the room and one thing leads to another....

Allison Baker—Assistant to Eloise Vale and part-time law student, this bashful woman decides to wear a slinky dress to her first party in ages. One look at the gorgeous man across the ballroom, and Allison's heart starts to hammer.

Eloise Vale—As Manhattan Multiples' director and a mother of triplet boys she finds enough to keep her busy. But her stomach is in knots because of continuous threats from a former flame, who is only the most powerful man in the city!

Bill Harper—With an empire to rule, the mayor of New York City has enough on his mind without memories of Eloise Vale, the only woman he's ever loved. And now she's the enemy. Can he find a way to bridge the gap between them? Find out next month in PRINCE OF THE CITY, by Nikki Benjamin (SE #1575).

Chapter One

"You're going to this party with us tonight."

Allison Baker didn't respond to Zoe's announcement. Instead she took a sip of iced tea, stretched out her legs, propped her bare feet on the yellow cushioned seat of the kitchen chair opposite her and smiled fondly at her friend.

Zoe Armbruster stopped pacing the floor and planted her hands on her hips, fixing Allison with a militant look. "Don't give me that sweet smile. I know you're thinking up a thousand excuses not to go. And I'm not buying any of them."

Allison gestured at the stacks of law books, legal tablets, pens and loose papers scattered over the small kitchen table. "Zoe, I'd love to go out with you and Jack, but I have to finish researching a legal brief for class next week."

Zoe held up a hand as if she were stopping traffic on a busy Manhattan street. "Nope. No excuses accepted. None. Zero. Zip. Nada." She caught Allison's hand and tugged her upright, spun her around and determinedly nudged her toward the bedroom. "You live the life of a nun—all work and no play. Tonight we're going to forget our daytime jobs and concentrate on having fun."

Laughing, Allison let Zoe urge her into the bedroom. The petite brunette was difficult to resist in this mood. Allison knew she should be looking for a case law to buttress the arguments in *State v. Cunningham,* but the prospect of a night away from law books and class assignments was tantalizing.

"I have absolutely nothing to wear to a society fund-raiser, Zoe." She sat on the end of the bed, her gaze following Zoe's curvy, shorts-clad figure as she slid back the closet door and began to push aside hangers. She glanced down at her own slim, five-foot, six-inch frame, then back at her friend's hourglass, five feet two inches of lush curves. "And there's no way I can wear anything of yours."

Zoe frowned at a tailored black business suit and pushed the padded hanger aside. "We'll find something. If we have to, we can always take in one of my dresses for you."

Allison laughed out loud. "That would take all night. We'd never make it to the party."

Zoe half disappeared into the back of the closet, her voice muffled. "You're going to this party if I have to steal a dress for you from Saks!"

"Oh, great," Allison said wryly, shaking her head and brushing back a lock of auburn hair that clung to her cheek. "You're willing to become a felon so I can attend a party?"

"Yes." Zoe's emphatic response was followed by a crow of satisfaction. She backed out of the closet, flourishing a clear plastic garment bag holding a lacy black gown. "Aha!"

Allison straightened. She'd forgotten about the designer gown, bought during a whirlwind shopping trip with her mother on her last visit to her parents' home in Beverly Hills. She'd never actually worn the dress because she'd flown back to Manhattan a day early to avoid accompanying her parents to a movie premiere. She hated the media frenzy that always attended her parents' appearances at the Hollywood parties they loved.

She'd managed to avoid attending any of the glamorous events since she was seventeen. That disastrous night at a film award after-party had left an indelible and traumatic imprint on her life.

Zoe unzipped the clear plastic bag and pulled out the gown, her eyes rounding. "Wow, this is great.

And absolutely perfect for tonight.'' She glanced at Allison. ''Do you have shoes to wear with it?''

''Yes. I think they're on the shelf behind a stack of winter sweaters.''

''Great! Here.'' Zoe tossed the dress at Allison and disappeared into the closet once more.

Allison smoothed her palm over the lace-covered satin, the rich material cool against her thighs, bare below the hem of her white shorts.

Zoe popped out of the closet, triumphantly dangling a pair of black strappy sandals from one hand. ''Here they are.'' She halted in front of Allison. ''Are you going to shower and dress quickly, or do I have to threaten you?''

''No, I give up.'' Allison laughed at the quick, mischievous smile that lit Zoe's face. ''I'll go to the party.''

An hour later Allison stared at her reflection in the long mirror that hung on the inside of the small bedroom door. Gone was the efficient personal assistant cum law student. The mirror reflected an image so unlike her daytime persona that it was startling. The black lace-over-satin gown clung to her slim curves, emphasizing the swell of her breasts below the off-the-shoulder neckline.

The narrow, ankle-length skirt was split up the side to just below midthigh, revealing the silk-clad length of pale thigh and calf, ending in black sandals with stiletto heels.

She turned, peering over her shoulder at the back of the dress. Black lace clung to the curve of hip and derriere with a subtle seductiveness. She'd caught up her hair and anchored it with simple gold combs, leaving wispy curls to brush against her temples and the nape of her neck. A single, twisted-gold chain encircled her throat, falling just above her collarbone. The matching gold-filigree earrings lent a touch of the exotic.

Subtle mascara and golden-brown eyeshadow gave her eyes a smoky, mysterious look accentuated by mocha-pink lipstick and blush.

The woman in the mirror didn't look cautious. She didn't look studious. She didn't look shy or introverted. She didn't look the slightest bit like Allison's normal self.

She looked, Allison thought, like a woman to be reckoned with, sure of herself, outgoing.

She curved her mouth into a smile. The woman in the mirror smiled back.

Allison smiled more widely.

Just for tonight, she told the woman in the mirror with uncharacteristic recklessness, *this is who I'm going to be. No yesterday, no tomorrow. Just tonight. I'm going to laugh and flirt and have fun.*

"Wow, look at you!" Zoe's reflection joined Allison's. "And look at the two of us—the Princess and Rose Red."

Zoe wore a crimson cocktail dress, her dark hair

and vibrant coloring a perfect foil for Allison's black lace, fair skin and auburn hair.

Allison linked her arm through Zoe's and tilted her head to one side, her laughing gaze pretending to assess their reflections. "Not bad for a secretary and a waitress, eh?"

Zoe waved her hand with airy unconcern. "I'm not a waitress, I'm a barista. And you're not a secretary, you're an executive's personal assistant on her way to becoming a brilliant attorney. And tonight," she added loftily, "we're both elegant ladies of society." The doorbell rang, interrupting her. "Oops, there's Jack."

Arm still linked with Allison's, Zoe hurried them out of the bedroom. Allison managed to catch up her tiny black evening bag and coat as they left the apartment.

The ballroom was so crowded that Allison was separated from Zoe and her date within minutes of their arrival. For once, however, she didn't mind being alone in a crowd. Wrapped safely in the protective trappings of a more glamorous and self-assured woman, she chatted easily with a much younger man standing beside her at the buffet table. He was obviously interested in her and she walked away from the encounter with her confidence soaring.

I'm a completely different person, she thought, smiling to herself. *This is such fun.*

The ballroom was decorated in a deep-sea theme, with Mediterranean-blue chiffon draped on the ceiling and covering the walls. Golden light gleamed softly through the filmy fabric, creating the illusion that the ballroom floated underwater. Spaced around the perimeter of the room were sculptures and photos of whales in their natural environment. In front of each display, clusters of guests gathered around professional lecturers who wore name tags and answered questions about sea life in general and whales in particular. Allison sipped champagne and wandered from group to group, fascinated by the depth and passion of the professors' responses to questions.

Standing on the edge of a group and listening to an oceanographer describe his group's efforts to return an orphaned baby whale to his pod in the waters off British Columbia, Allison stiffened at the whisper-light brush of fingers against her nape.

Startled, she spun to confront whomever had touched her, but found no one. She stood at the edge of the group, and though the room was crowded, no one was within arm's reach.

How odd. Puzzled, she turned back to the lecturer.

Within moments she felt that same brush against her nape. Frowning, she glanced over her shoulder.

But again no one stood close enough to have touched her.

Her gaze swept the crowd and she went perfectly still.

Across the packed ballroom, a man leaned against a marble pillar, watching her.

Allison felt his intense black gaze as surely as if he'd reached out, slipped his arm around her waist and pulled her body against his. He was tall and very tan, Hispanic perhaps, with short black hair and eyes so dark they seemed black.

She couldn't tear her gaze from his, and it wasn't until the crowd shifted, blocking her view of him, that she drew a deep breath and realized she had been staring. She sipped her champagne and glanced about her, relieved when no one seemed to have noticed her preoccupation. Flustered and suddenly much too warm, she walked quickly through the open French doors behind her and out onto the stone terrace.

Allison leaned on the balustrade, drawing deep, calming breaths and gazing out at the lights of the city below her.

The last place Jorge Perez wanted to be on a hot Saturday night in August was at a fund-raiser for a save-the-whales organization. Not that he didn't want to save whales from extinction. He would gladly have written a hefty check and donated to the cause. His objection was to the party itself. He rarely attended society events, preferring to spend his weekends working, but when his boss had asked him to stand in for him, Jorge couldn't refuse. He liked Ross and he doted on Ross's two kids, Ben and Sarah. When the children cornered him and begged him to go in Ross's stead so their father could take them sailing for the weekend, he'd given in.

So here he was, dressed in an Armani tux instead of faded jeans, chatting with city council members, sidestepping the not-so-subtle advances of a Hollywood starlet hanging off the arm of a local hotel tycoon, and fielding questions from a *Times* reporter about the details of the latest murder case.

What a way to spend the weekend.

He glanced at his Rolex and calculated that he ought to circulate for another thirty minutes before he could legitimately tell his hostess good-night without being considered rude.

Behind him he heard the starlet's tinkling laugh, and he swallowed a groan. Without looking over his shoulder, he eased around the laughing group ahead of him, snagged a champagne glass from a passing waiter and kept walking until he reached the relative safety of the back wall. He leaned his shoulder against a convenient marble pillar and let his gaze drift over the room.

He recognized many of the people from the days

when his ex-fiancée had dragged him to parties like this one several times a week. The engagement hadn't lasted and neither had his regular attendance at this sort of function.

Bored, he glanced idly over the throng, mentally ticking off minutes. The crowd shifted and abruptly parted to frame a woman directly across the huge room. Boredom fled, his attention caught, riveted by the sight of her. Auburn hair gleamed beneath the subtle gold lighting, her shape willowy inside a slim tube of black lace. She stood with her back to him, and he silently willed her to turn. He needed to see her face.

Come on, he urged silently. *Turn around.*

When she did, he felt sucker-punched, his muscles tightening with a swift rush of adrenaline.

She was incredibly beautiful. In a room filled with expensive, manicured, designer-dressed and jewel-draped gorgeous women, she stood out like a glowing candle. Black lace cupped shoulders that gleamed ivory above the low neckline, her throat a slim column accented by a single strand of gold. Wisps of auburn hair curled against temple, cheek and nape, while the rest of the rich, deep red mass was caught up in a loose gathering of curls that looked about to tumble to her shoulders with her slightest movement.

She turned away, facing the lecturer, and the movement shifted her dress, exposing the length of her thigh and calf, pale against the shimmering black of her skirt.

Who the hell is she? Jorge knew most of the people in the room, if not by sight, then by reputation. He was sure he'd never seen the beautiful redhead before. He would have remembered.

The crowd shifted yet again, cutting off his view of her.

Come on. Come on. He stared at the slice of auburn hair and black dress still visible and willed the chattering throng to move apart.

The laughing, gossiping crowd moved again, groups splitting apart and reforming, the floor of the ballroom reflecting the ebb and flow of the sea the decorator had sought to replicate.

She came into view again. Muscles tense with anticipation, he waited for her to turn and look at him. She glanced over her shoulder, a tiny frown between her brows as her gaze swept the crowd as if searching for someone.

Her gaze met his. Jorge felt the connection as surely as if an electrical current surged between them. He couldn't tell what color her eyes were from this distance, but he saw them widen, saw her body go still.

He bit off a curse as the crowd shifted, blocking his view of her, and he pushed away from the pillar to make his way across the crowded floor. Closer now, he realized that she'd left the group clustered around the lecturer. Swiftly he scanned the crowd, catching a glimpse of auburn hair as she slipped through the French doors onto the terrace. He quickly altered direction, moving around the perimeter of the room, briefly pausing to collect a nearly full bottle of champagne and two flutes from a friendly waiter before stepping out onto the terrace.

He saw her immediately. She leaned against the balustrade, head tilted back, gazing up at the night sky. Standing just outside the soft circle of light cast by the French doors, the black of her gown nearly blended into the shadows. The fair skin of throat, shoulder, arms and face, however, gleamed pale against the darker night.

Jorge moved slowly toward her, taking the opportunity to observe before being seen.

"It's too bad we can't see the stars."

She went still. Then she turned her head, looking over her shoulder at him.

Her eyes were amber, smoky as well-aged scotch, and filled with a wariness that belied the sophistication of the black lace gown and upswept hair.

Jorge immediately abandoned any thought of glib pickup lines.

Even before she looked over her shoulder and met his dark gaze, instinct told Allison that the deep drawl belonged to the man from the ballroom. For one moment, sheer panic threatened to engulf her.

But then he smiled, the corners of his eyes crinkling, the nearly black irises reflecting the warmth of his smile, and the grip of fear that often accompanied her dealings with men eased.

He moved closer, halting a decorous four feet away, and looked up at the sky.

"Air pollution," he commented.

"Air pollution?"

His gaze met hers briefly before returning to the dome of hazy, not-quite-dark sky. He gestured at the city below and around them, the soft glow of lamplight from inside the ballroom glinting briefly off the crystal flutes in his hand.

"Maybe it's more accurate to call it light pollution." He took a step nearer, leaned one hip against the balustrade and handed her a flute, then filled it. "Did you know that the astronauts only see the darkness of night in the less populated sections of the United States, like North Dakota or Montana? On the east and west coasts the population is so dense and the use of electricity so high that astronauts see them lit up at night, not dark."

"Really?" Allison sipped her champagne, tense muscles slowly relaxing as he continued to lean casually against the low stone edge and made no attempt to close the distance between them. He was tall, well over six feet, his shoulders wide beneath the black jacket of his tuxedo.

"Really." He grinned, the corners of his mouth

curving upward, his eyes laughing at her. "Are you interested in astronomy?"

"Um…" Allison realized that she was staring in fascination at the curve of his lips and had no clue what he'd said. "I beg your pardon?"

"Astronomy," he said gently. "Are you an astronomy fan?"

"I was as a child, but I haven't had time for stargazing since I moved to New York," she responded absentmindedly, wondering if the golden tone of his skin was natural or if he spent a lot of time outdoors.

"And how long ago was that?"

"Several years." Allison suddenly realized that he was asking questions and she was answering without thought because she was so fascinated by him. Each time he smiled at her, she was more aware of the slow, heavy throb of her pulse and the swift kick of sexual attraction. For the first time in her life, she found herself physically attracted to a man. Even more startling was her complete lack of fear. She felt oddly safe with him. He's the perfect man to flirt with, she realized, remembering her earlier promise to the woman in the mirror. *Tonight I'm going to flirt and have fun.*

She smiled in anticipation. He smiled back, his gaze narrowing, growing more intense.

"I'm afraid I've forgotten to introduce myself,"

she said politely, holding out her hand. "I'm Allison Baker."

"Pleased to meet you, Allison." He took her hand in his and stepped closer. "I'm Jorge."

His hand engulfed hers, the fingers and palm faintly rough, his warmth and the touch of skin against skin sending prickles of awareness zinging through her body.

"Hello." Her voice was throaty, husky with the force of her emotions.

His eyes darkened, his fingers tightening over hers.

"So, tell me, Allison Baker." He smoothed his thumb over the back of her hand. "What's a nice girl like you doing in a place like this?"

He quirked a dark eyebrow, his teeth flashing in a teasing grin, and Allison laughed.

"You mean on this particular terrace, or at a save-the-whales fund-raiser?"

"Whichever. Mostly, I'm just wondering if you have a particular affinity for whales."

"Ah, you're wondering if I'm attracted to large mammals?"

He chuckled, the sound a deep growl of amusement. Before he could respond, the French doors flew open behind them and a wave of chattering party guests spilled out onto the terrace. The orchestra music followed them, and several couples began to dance.

Jorge glanced over his shoulder at the noisy crowd and the whirling couples. "I think the party has found us." He took the flute from her hand and set both hers and his next to the nearly empty bottle of champagne on the balustrade. "It's a shame to waste the music. Shall we?"

Allison nodded, and he slipped an arm around her waist to tug her body gently against his. He folded his fingers around her right hand and swept her into the rhythm.

She felt the same jolt of startled recognition that she'd felt in the ballroom earlier, when she'd looked up and found him watching her. The black silk of her bodice brushed against his pleated white shirt, her left hand lay against the black tux jacket covering his broad shoulder and only inches from the thick dark hair that gleamed in the light from the ballroom behind them. Each time she drew breath, she pulled in the subtle scent of his after-shave. Spicy and masculine, it mingled with an underlying hint of clean soap, starched shirt and a uniquely male scent in a potent, heady mix that went straight to her blood, making it race more swiftly through her veins.

"Tell me, Allison Baker, what do you do when you're not dazzling men at fund-raisers for large mammals?"

She tilted her head back, her lips curving in response to his teasing smile. Should she tell him about her job at Manhattan Multiples? No, she decided, not tonight. *Tonight, I'm not my everyday self.* So she compromised. "I'm a student."

"Really? And what are you studying?"

"Law."

"Yet another thing we have in common." The music changed, switching to a slower tune. They swayed in time to the music, and he lifted her right hand to his shoulder so he could clasp her waist and draw her nearer.

"You're studying law, also?"

"No. I did study law, now I practice law."

She beamed at him, delighted. "You're an attorney? How lovely. What field do you specialize in?"

"Criminal law."

"Then you must be very busy," she said dryly. "The crime rate in America is a disgrace."

"Hey," he laughed. "Not my fault. And I'm doing my part to improve the situation."

A waiter moved past them, circulating a tray of canapes, and Jorge skillfully avoided a collision by tucking Allison closer. Their bodies pressed together from shoulder to thigh and she caught her breath, blindsided by the surge of desire that had her slipping her arms around his neck to hold him closer. His arms tightened, crushing her against him.

Allison was only vaguely aware that the sounds of music and laughter faded; she was too caught up in the feel of his hard body against her softer curves and in the driving need to have more. She tilted her head back to look up at him, her hair brushing against his throat and face, and found his eyes glittering down at her between lowered lashes.

Then his mouth covered hers, and the sexual tension that had vibrated between them from the first, exploded. She was dizzy with it, her heart pounding frantically, heat exploding in her veins.

The kiss quickly skipped all the tentative preliminaries of a first embrace and went straight to carnal. One big hand cradled the back of her head and his tongue thrust against hers as he ravaged her mouth. Delight raced through her veins and she met him eagerly, gasping with shock that quickly submerged beneath sheer pleasure as his hand covered the black silk over her breast and found the stiff peak of her nipple. He pushed her against the wall and shifted, pressing one hard thigh between her legs.

She murmured frantically, twisting against him in an unsuccessful attempt to find release. For one heartstopping moment he surged against her, but then he stiffened, the muscles in his arms flexing with iron strength before he pulled his mouth from hers, breathing hard.

"Allison, we can't do this here. Come upstairs with me."

She stared at him, unable to think, the transition

from total absorption in the physical to clear thought impossible.

''I have a room upstairs. Ross booked it for himself and his wife—when he asked me to stand in for him tonight, he gave me the key in case I wanted to stay over. Come upstairs with me, sweetheart. Please.'' His voice was nearly unrecognizable, roughened with the passion that vibrated between them.

''I don't do this sort of thing,'' she finally managed to say, not sure why it was so important for him to know.

The heat in his eyes flared, the pupils black with desire. ''Neither do I.''

Allison could barely think with his hard body pressed against hers and her own body screaming to continue. She'd never felt passion before, had never thought she would, not after being forced by a date when she was barely seventeen. Could she turn her back on what might be her one chance to make love?

Just for tonight, she thought. Just this once.

''Yes.''

Fierce satisfaction blazed in his eyes. Without another word he stepped back, wrapping an arm around her when her legs wobbled.

She hesitated, holding a hand to her hair. ''Do we have to go through the ballroom?'' she murmured, glancing about them and realizing for the first time that they stood in the shelter of a heavy stone column, out of sight of the other guests.

"No." He flicked an assessing glance over her and tugged her bodice higher over the swell of her breasts, his fingers reluctantly leaving the soft skin. "There's a back way."

He took her through a nearly hidden door at the far end of the terrace that led to a service hallway behind the huge ballroom. Tucked against his side, Allison was soon confused by the maze of corridors they walked through to reach the elevator.

"How do you know so much about this hotel?" she asked as the elevator rose.

"They were robbed two years ago. I prosecuted the case and spent a lot of time walking the halls and studying the layout to understand the system the defendants used."

She nodded, barely listening to his words, her gaze focused on the movement of his lips as he spoke. She badly wanted his mouth on hers.

"Stop it." The growled words were thick. When her gaze met his, his eyes were hot. "I'm not going to touch you in here. If I do, we won't make it to the room."

Her mouth formed a startled, rounded *O*. His arm tightened around her shoulder, tension thickening the air, the hard body she was tucked against strung taut with control.

The elevator doors opened silently, and Jorge

moved her out and down the hallway with swift purpose. One quick swipe of the card key opened the door, and within seconds they were inside. He backed her against the door and took her mouth, his hands making short work of the zipper at the back of her gown. Allison helped him, wiggling impatiently as he pushed the dress off her shoulders, his mouth leaving hers to find the peak of her breast as the dress pooled around her feet.

She screamed when he tugged her nipple into the hot, wet cave of his mouth and sucked, her hips pressing urgently against his.

He swore and picked her up, crossing to the bed. Within seconds he'd stripped both of them, donned protection and covered her. She welcomed the heavy, hot press of his weight, nearly mindless as he drove her higher with his hands and mouth.

He lifted above her, going motionless, his dark hair tousled, the lines of his face fiercely possessive. "Are you safe?"

Allison could barely understand his words, his voice thick and roughened. What had he said? Was she safe? The answer was yes; she felt safe with a male for the first time in her life. She nodded, unable to speak, and then she forgot all about safety for he surged inside her and sent them both over the edge.

Allison frowned and flipped the page on her desk calendar again.

This can't be right.

But there was no getting around the fact that the last time she'd scribbled red asterisks on her calendar to mark the beginning and end of her monthly period was over six weeks ago.

Did I forget?

No, she knew she hadn't forgotten. She never forgot to jot down the dates of her period. She'd been jotting those little red marks on her calendars since the summer she turned thirteen.

She quickly scanned the notations on the days between the last little red mark and today's date. Halfway in between, she was stopped short by a date, circled in red but without an accompanying note; it was the Saturday night she'd gone to the party with Zoe and Jack—and left with Jorge Perez.

Heat moved through her veins and flushed her face and she squeezed her eyes closed at the flood of memories. They'd spent hours together after leaving the party. *I shouldn't have slept with him.* But sleeping had nothing to do with what the two of them had done in his bed.

Allison dropped her face into her hands and groaned.

I'm such an idiot. What was I thinking?

She hadn't been thinking, she admitted to herself. That was the problem. She hadn't been able to think rationally from the moment she'd looked across the ballroom and found him watching her. And when he took her in his arms, their powerful sexual attraction drove everything but him from her mind.

It wasn't until she'd wakened in the gray predawn that she asked herself what came next—and then she'd panicked, slipped from his bed and fled the hotel room. She hadn't seen him since; but then, she hadn't expected to. He didn't know where she lived or worked and in a city as large as New York, it was unlikely that he would find her, even if he bothered to search, which she doubted he would.

She flipped the calendar page to the current month, absentmindedly jotting "six weeks" on the square for today's date.

I hope I don't start my period this weekend, she thought idly. She had too much homework to finish and she couldn't afford to spend a day in bed with cramps.

She stared at the red letters she'd just written on the white square. Six weeks? Of course, she thought, frowning. It had been six weeks. Something about the time frame niggled at the edge of her consciousness. *But I'm never late.*

Her hand froze, the tip of the fountain pen bleeding a small spreading blob of red ink on to the pristine white paper of the calendar. Allison stared at the red blot without seeing it, horror widening her eyes and shortening her breath.

Six weeks—my period is two weeks overdue. Could I be pregnant?

A swift image of Jorge Perez's compelling face and the muscled strength of his body pressing hers into rumpled sheets had her groaning with dawning apprehension and shock.

Pregnancy was more than a possibility, she realized. She wasn't on the pill, nor had she used a diaphragm or any other form of contraception. That night with Jorge was the first time in her life she'd been carried away by passion, and she'd been completely unprepared.

She knew that condoms had a risk factor. She couldn't even blame Jorge if she'd conceived that night, because he'd used protection. She was the one who'd been irresponsible and failed to add backup birth control.

She dropped the pen on the calendar and sat back, pushing trembling fingers through the thick fall of her hair.

What am I going to do if I'm pregnant?

Her hand pressed against her belly in an instinctive, protective gesture.

Her one night of incredible passion with Jorge might have consequences that would alter her life forever. Not to mention her body.

She tilted her chin down and stared assessingly at her torso. She couldn't discern any changes—her abdomen was as flat as usual.

But if she were pregnant, the shape of her body wouldn't stay the same for long. She'd seen lots of pregnant women come and go through the doors of Manhattan Multiples, a care center for mothers expecting more than a single baby, and she had no illusions about what would happen to her now-slender body if she were carrying Jorge's baby.

Jorge. She blanched. Did she have to tell him?

Of course I have to tell him. How can I not?

On the other hand, how could she? Would he be happy? Angry? Would he want visitation rights, or God forbid, custody?

Allison pressed a hand to her chest, felt the heavy thud of her racing heart, and took several deep breaths in an effort to calm herself.

She had to be practical, she thought, forcing herself to think logically, when she really wanted to run screaming from the building. Before she considered all the many questions, she had to find out if she was really pregnant. On her lunch hour she would go to the pharmacy and buy a pregnancy kit.

She glanced at her watch. Two hours until lunch.

Resolutely she shifted her calendar to the corner of her desk and pulled a file toward her, flipping it open. She forced herself to focus, bringing up the appropriate data file on her computer and moving doggedly through the necessary action.

She canceled a lunch date with a co-worker and went to the pharmacy instead, returning with the kit concealed in a plain brown bag tucked into her purse. The afternoon hours dragged by, the hour hand on her watch moving slowly toward 5:00 p.m.

The hum of activity in the office grew louder with end-of-the-day preparations, drawers opening and slamming shut, files being dropped into the return-to-shelf basket.

"Don't work too late, Allison."

Allison lifted her head to find her boss, Eloise Vale, standing in her office doorway, her purse slung over one shoulder and a leather briefcase in her hand.

"I won't."

"Good. You spend too many late nights in the office," Eloise chided, her smile affectionate.

"Not tonight. I promise."

"I'll hold you to that." Eloise glanced at her watch. "Oh, drat. I'm going to be late. Bye."

Allison called a good-night as Eloise whisked off down the hall. She forced herself to wait until all sounds had ceased, until the last slam of desk drawers being closed and cheery good-nights were followed by the closing of the outer door. Then she made herself wait another ten minutes in case one of her office mates had forgotten something and might return to their desks.

At last, reassured by the absence of human activity in the silent outer office, she picked up her purse and left her office for the community bathroom.

The room was silent. Allison pushed open the

doors to the three empty stalls to verify that she was alone before dropping her purse on to the marble-topped vanity. A crystal vase with a bouquet of spicy, white carnations, lush pink roses and delicate white baby's breath brightened one corner of the gray marble countertop that held two sinks with porcelain fittings. Recessed lamps cast a soft light in front of the long mirror that took up the entire wall above the vanity.

Allison drew in a deep breath, flipped open her purse and closed her fingers over the brown-bag-enclosed test kit.

The door flew open with a bang. She jumped, startled, and spun to find the white-haired janitor, who looked every bit as surprised as Allison felt.

"Oh, my goodness!" The janitor's hand flew to his heart and he audibly caught his breath. "I'm sorry, ma'am—I didn't know anyone was here. I'll come back later...."

"No." Allison curved her lips upward in a stiff smile. "No, I'm finished."

She edged her way past the elderly man and his cart of cleaning supplies and walked back down the hall to her office. Leaving the door open wide, she sat at her desk and turned on her computer, staring blindly at the glowing screen. The minutes seemed to crawl by. At last she heard the rattle of the cart as the janitor left the rest room and moved off down the hall. Allison forced herself to wait until the sound of wastebaskets clattering against the trash can ceased, until the music from the portable radio clipped to the wheeled cart faded, until the outer door to the offices clicked shut. Silence reigned once more.

Allison picked up her purse and crossed to the doorway, peering cautiously out into the hall. Nothing stirred. For the second time, she left her office and moved quickly down the hall to the rest room. She flipped on the lights, crossed to the vanity and pulled out the test kit.

Scant moments later she stared at the stick. There were two little windows, one a little circle, the other a little square. Both of them had a pink line. The test result was positive.

I'm pregnant.

She couldn't stop staring at the pink lines in their small windows. In an unconsciously protective gesture, her hand lifted to rest on the flat plane of her abdomen.

Her gaze followed the movement of her hand, searching for any change in her body beneath her fingers.

Nothing. She looked just as she always did.

She wondered frantically if she could ignore the pregnancy.

Oh, right. That's a great plan. The functioning, practical side of her brain scoffed at the ridiculous idea.

Her gaze lifted and she stared at her reflection, dazed, her stunned mind struggling to grasp the fact that in eight months she would give birth.

She had to have a plan. She stared at her reflection in the mirror, overwhelmed by the concept of the tiny life growing inside her. How would she cope with a baby? She didn't know anything about being a mother. And how could she work at the office all day, go to school at night and still have time to care for a child? But how would she support them if she didn't finish law school? The barrage of scattered, panicked questions hit her like a tidal wave until she felt light-headed.

She braced her palms on the vanity edge and bent forward to lower her head. Her hair swung forward to brush against her cheeks, and she closed her eyes until the dizziness passed.

At last she opened her eyes and cautiously lifted her head, eyeing her reflection in the mirror. The soft lighting was kind, but there was no denying that her cheeks were pale, her eyes dark and bruised looking. Feeling faintly nauseated, Allison ran trembling fingers through her hair, pushing it back from her face.

I can't make decisions now, she acknowledged. The only thing she knew for sure was that she was keeping this baby. Determination firmed her chin and once again, she smoothed her palm over her flat tummy. She'd give herself a few days to think about all the probabilities, then make choices and plans.

In the meantime, she thought, she'd have to conceal her worry from her darling, but very snoopy, boss. Eloise had sharp eyes and was genuinely interested in the well-being of all her employees at Manhattan Multiples. Allison knew that she would have to be very good at hiding her distraction. She only hoped that she would have a few weeks before her growing tummy became so obvious that Eloise guessed her secret.

The same day that Allison was struggling to come to terms with the shocking confirmation of her pregnancy, Jorge worked late at the office and returned to his apartment after 10:00 p.m.

He stopped in the kitchen and pulled open the refrigerator door to grab a bottle of water before heading down the dark hall to the second bedroom that he'd converted into an office. Dropping his briefcase and suit jacket on the leather recliner, he crossed to the desk, switched on the lamp, and pushed the on button for the laptop computer sitting atop the polished mahogany. While he waited for it to boot up, he opened the water bottle and drank as he picked up messages from the fax machine. Halfway through the small stack of paper, he halted, his attention captured by the distinctive letterhead of the Bretton Detective Agency. He dropped the rest of the papers back into the fax machine tray, a fierce surge of anticipation flooding him as he quickly read the body of the message.

The Bretton detective had found her. The black-and-white copy of the faxed photo attached to the letter was grainy, but there was no question that the woman glancing over her shoulder as she entered a shop was Allison Baker. And she not only lived across town, she worked in the city.

Jorge glanced at the clock and muttered a curse. It was too late to appear on her doorstep.

But he had her work address. He'd see her tomorrow.

"Manhattan Multiples." He wondered briefly what the company did. The detective's report listed the company name and Allison's job title as personal assistant, but there was no indication as to what type of business Manhattan Multiples was engaged in.

He jotted a quick note to the detective agency confirming that the photo was indeed the Allison Baker he wanted to find and requested a final bill.

He knew the search was going to be expensive, but finding Allison was worth whatever it cost. He could have asked the police detective assigned to the district attorney's office to run a search for her, but to do so would have required him to explain why he wanted her located. And he wasn't willing to tell anyone that spending one night with the elusive redhead had left him craving her so badly that he was willing to turn the city upside down in order to see her again.

And when I see her, he thought grimly, she's going to explain why she ran away and left me alone in that damn hotel room without saying good-bye or leaving me a note. How the hell did she think he was going to see her again?

Probably because she didn't want to see me again.

The knowledge ate at him, corrosive as acid. Despite the likelihood that Allison hadn't planned to ever contact him, Jorge couldn't let it go. He'd felt something rare and powerful that night. Until she told him face-to-face that she hadn't felt it, too, he wasn't giving up.

Chapter Two

The morning after her positive pregnancy test, Allison was at her desk at the usual hour. Instead of downing her customary mug of coffee, however, she frowned at the steaming black brew and slowly returned the mug to her desk, untouched.

Was it safe for the baby if she drank coffee with caffeine?

She had no idea.

She'd buy some books at lunch and research prenatal care. She moved the mug of coffee to the far corner of her desk, gave it one last, longing glance and flipped open a personnel file.

"Good morning, Allison."

Allison looked up. Eloise stood in the doorway, a steaming cup in one hand and a sheaf of papers in the other.

"Good morning, Eloise." She watched her boss glance up and down the hallway before moving quickly to the chair opposite her desk. The older woman's air of suppressed excitement roused Allison's curiosity. "What is it?"

"Someone on my staff is pregnant."

Allison felt her eyes widen. She was incapable of speech. For a long, fraught moment, all she could do was stare at Eloise.

"Pregnant?" she finally managed. "What makes you think one of the staff is pregnant?"

Eloise leaned forward, her excitement palpable. "I found a used pregnancy kit in the staff bathroom this morning and the stick had a positive reading."

"Oh." Frantically, Allison tried to remember if she'd forgotten anything else in the ladies rest room besides the pregnancy kit. How could she have been so careless? Had she left anything else that would lead Eloise to her?

"I can't imagine who it could be, can you?"

Fortunately for Allison, Eloise didn't pause long enough for an answer.

"It can't be Leah, because she's already pregnant." Her lips pursed as she paused, clearly considering the rest of her staff. "Where to start, that's the question. We must have nearly twenty employees at the moment, don't we?"

"Yes, if we count part-time as well as full-time staff."

"Hmmm." Eloise tapped the tip of one elegant, manicured nail against her chin. "I'm determined to find out who among us is pregnant."

"I'm sure you'll know soon. It's not likely that a pregnancy can be concealed for long, is it?" Allison asked.

"That's true. Still, it's a mystery, and you know how I feel about mysteries."

"Yes, I do." Despite her worry, Allison couldn't help smiling with affection at Eloise, who was animated with curiosity. *I need a diversion, something to refocus Eloise's attention.* She glanced at the file on her desk. "Speaking of mysteries, are my eyes deceiving me, or did you hire twins as our new security guards?"

"I did."

"How did you find them? And however are we going to tell them apart?"

Eloise laughed. She stood and leaned across the desk to look at the photos clipped to the two new personnel files that Allison was assembling. "I suppose we'll have to make name tags so we can tell which one is Tony Martino and which is his brother, Frank. They're great-looking guys, aren't they?"

"Yes, they are." Allison thought that "great-looking" didn't adequately do justice to the pair of well-muscled, black-haired, brown-eyed brothers. They looked like definite heartbreakers. "Which brother is working day shift?"

"Tony. And Frank will work nights. Actually, that will help solve the problem of knowing which brother we're talking to, since they won't be working during the same hours."

"True." The phone rang and Allison answered it, listened a moment, then held the receiver out to Eloise. "It's for you. Leah says it's the federal grant writer you've been trying to reach."

"At last! The file is on my desk, ask Leah to transfer the call, will you please?" Eloise barely waited for Allison's nod before she turned and hurried out the door.

Allison relayed her request to the receptionist and drew a deep breath of relief as the door closed behind her boss.

That was a close call. How could she have been so careless as to leave the test kit in the bathroom? She propped her elbows on the desktop and covered her face with her hands. Thank goodness her boss didn't seem to give a thought to the possibility that she might be the mysterious pregnant person.

The quick rap of knuckles on her office door startled her, and Allison sat bolt upright, running a quick, smoothing hand over her hair.

"Yes?"

The door opened and Leah Simpson appeared, her very round, thoroughly pregnant midsection preceding her over the threshold.

"There's someone here to see you, Allison."

"There is?" Allison checked her calendar, but no name was jotted in the current time slot. "I don't have any appointments scheduled this morning. Who is it?"

Leah rolled her eyes and pretended to fan herself with one hand. Beneath her blond hair, her hazel eyes sparkled with mischief.

"He wouldn't give me his name."

"Why not?"

"He said he wanted to surprise you."

Curiouser and curiouser. "What does he look like?" She stood, flipping the page of her calendar to verify that she hadn't inadvertently noted an appointment on the wrong day.

"He's tall, over six feet, great body, black hair, brown eyes," Leah recited. "And he's sexy as sin."

Allison's world stood still. *It can't be him.* It just couldn't be true that Jorge Perez was in the outer office expecting to see her. Not today, of all days.

"Allison? Should I show him in?"

Before Allison could think of a reason to say no, the deep, molasses-smooth male voice that she'd been hearing in her dreams for the past four weeks, answered for her.

"No need, I'll show myself in."

Jorge appeared in the doorway just behind Leah. Allison would have groaned aloud if she'd been capable of making any noise at all. She was so stunned to see him, however, that all she could do was stare, speechless, held immobile by his intense gaze.

She was barely aware that Leah quickly excused herself, so focused was she on Jorge. He looked away, stepping aside to allow Leah to exit and flashing the charming smile that transformed his face from remote to irresistible. Allison's heart clenched, the sheer, helpless pleasure of seeing him again made painful by the knowledge that she'd bolted from his bed and hotel room without saying goodbye. It was really not a good excuse that she was totally unschooled in the proper etiquette of handling the morning after great sex and that she'd simply panicked. He had every right to be annoyed with her.

In the few short moments that his attention was diverted by Leah, she indulged herself by openly staring, absorbing all the small details about him. He was just as devastating in a dark-gray tailored suit, white shirt and tie as he had been in formal evening clothes at the fund-raiser. His shoulders were just as broad; his skin equally tanned against

the white of his shirt collar; and his black hair shone
with the sheen of a raven's wing under the office
lighting.

He closed the door and turned to face her. Allison gathered her dignity around her like a cloak and
faced him with what she hoped was calm.

Jorge thought he'd be elated to see Allison, but
the surge of fierce emotion that he felt at first sight
of her was quickly replaced by a wave of anger just
as powerful.

"Hello, Allison."

"Hello, Jorge."

"You're looking well." Better than well, he
thought, temper rising. She was damn near glowing.
It was obvious that she hadn't been spending sleepless nights wondering where he was. Unlike him,
wondering about her. And unlike him, she was too
damn cool about seeing him after four long weeks.

"Thank you," she answered gravely. "So are
you."

He shoved his hands in his pockets and stepped
away from the door, looking around to survey the
room. "Nice office."

"Thank you," she said again. "What are you
doing here, Jorge?"

She sounded genuinely bewildered. He didn't
know whether to be offended or flattered. He raised
a brow. "I only recently learned where you worked,

and since I had an appointment in the neighborhood, decided to drop by and say hello.''

"Oh." She lifted a hand in unconscious appeal, then dropped her hand to her side. "I..."

He caught a glimpse of small white teeth as she bit her lip with indecision. Good, he thought savagely. It's nice to know that I'm not the only one unsure of myself.

He deliberately stared at her. Beginning at the silky crown of her head, his gaze moved lower, then slowly back up again. Gone was the passionate woman in the sexy black dress. In her place was a calm, cool woman in a tailored, caramel-colored suit, the neat white blouse she wore beneath the jacket buttoned demurely to her throat. Her hair, though, was the same vibrant shade of auburn, and her creamy skin glowed.

He frowned. Now that he looked more closely, he could see faint, bluish circles beneath her eyes, the gold depths darker, shadowed.

Probably with guilt for running out on me after she spent the night.

She shifted under his gaze, a faint pink tinting her cheeks, and he realized that he'd been standing motionless, silently staring at her for far too long. He tore his gaze from her face and glanced around the room. A group of framed photos hung on the wall nearest her desk, and he moved closer to study them.

"Friends of yours?" The older couple in the center photograph was vaguely familiar, but he couldn't place where he'd seen them before.

"My parents, actually."

"Mmm." The couple was featured in all of the photos, he realized. And he easily recognized the film, stage and political heavyweights that shared the shots. Comprehension dawned and he looked at Allison. "Baker? Your parents are Stephen and Marguerite Baker, the film producers?"

"Yes."

"You're just full of surprises, aren't you, Allison," he said softly.

She looked genuinely confused. She should have stayed in Hollywood and become an actress, he thought, furious. She's giving an Academy-Award-winning performance.

"I don't know what you mean."

"No?" Jorge knew that he'd just discovered why Allison hadn't contacted him. Her parents were rich and famous while he was the son of a blue-collar worker. Although he'd become a powerful man in Manhattan, his comfortable wealth and position were self-made, while Allison had been born into wealth in a talented, famous family. He'd encountered social snobbery before, but it hadn't occurred to him that prejudice was a possibility with Allison.

"Jorge, I know that our night together was a one-night aberration for you."

He blinked slowly, trying to follow her reasoning. "An aberration?"

"Of course. I read the newspaper society columns on occasion. I'm well aware that I'm not the sort of woman you normally date."

"Really?" He looked her swiftly up and down and shook his head, baffled.

She pushed nervous fingers through her hair and tucked it behind her ear before clasping her hands tightly together at her waist. "I know that I shouldn't have left the room that morning without saying goodbye. I certainly understand that you expected to hear from me, and that you're no doubt curious as to why I failed to contact you, but you needn't worry. I don't plan to pursue you."

"You don't?" *Why the hell not?*

"No. Let me assure you that I don't expect anything further from you."

Jorge drew a deep breath and forced his fingers to unclench. "What the hell are you talking about?" he said through his teeth, struggling to control the urge to grab her and shake her until her cool reserve shattered and the laughing, open woman he'd met on the terrace emerged.

"I want you to know that I understand our worlds are very different. That's why I didn't get in touch after..." She paused, her gaze chasing away from his before she drew a deep breath, lifted her chin and looked directly at him once more.

"After we spent the night together. And why I didn't stay around that morning to discuss it."

Before Jorge could respond, the intercom on her desk buzzed. She tapped the button on her phone, and a disembodied voice spoke.

"Eloise asked me to remind you that they're waiting for you in the conference room, Allison. The meeting with the city budget people, remember?"

"Thank you, Leah. Please tell her that I'm on my way."

She flicked off the intercom, glancing at Jorge as she bent to open a drawer and extract a file. "I'm sorry, Jorge, but I have to go to this meeting." She tucked the file under one arm, picked up a pen and rounded the desk to walk toward him. "Thank you for dropping by," she said politely, holding out her hand. "It was nice to see you."

Jorge took her hand, the soft touch of her skin against his creating an instant vision of all of her, naked, pressed against the length of him. Under him. Holding her gaze with his, he lifted her hand and pressed a kiss to her warm palm, lingering when her eyes widened.

She froze, then tugged on her hand until he reluctantly released her.

"I, um…" she paused, cleared her throat before continuing. "Have a nice day."

He smiled. She was clearly flustered, her cool

reserve in tatters from the touch of his lips against her palm. He reached past her, his arm brushing her sleeve, and pulled open the door. He didn't miss the slight, startled jerk of her body as they touched, and though it wasn't enough, not nearly enough, he decided to let her flee. This time.

"You too, Allison." Her wide gaze met his, questioning. "Have a good day."

"Oh. Yes. I will. Goodbye." She turned, hurrying out of the office and down the hall away from him.

It's not goodbye, sweetheart, not by a long shot. He watched her slim back, the skirt of her suit reaching a decorous two inches below her knees. It should be illegal to cover up those legs. The memory of kissing the backs of her knees before his lips moved higher haunted him, and was just as vivid now as it had been the day after that long, unforgettable night. He watched her until she disappeared through a door at the end of the hall. Then he turned and left the office complex, frustrated, impatient and so preoccupied with analyzing their conversation during those few moments in Allison's office that he didn't respond when Leah said goodbye.

Allison couldn't focus on the meeting.

She kept seeing Jorge, his polite words the complete opposite of the heat and anger churning in his dark eyes. Unsure of him and terrified that he'd somehow learned, or would learn, about her pregnancy, she'd drawn her customary cloak of cool reserve around her like a defense shield and taken refuge behind it.

Why had he come to her office?

How had he found her?

Why had he bothered to do either?

The questions had baffled her until she realized it was likely she was the first woman who hadn't pursued him after spending the night in his bed. When she assumed that his visit to her was quite possibly generated by curiosity, she'd tried to reassure him that she accepted theirs was a one-night-only event.

Strangely enough, he hadn't seemed relieved. In fact, he looked downright furious. And he'd seemed angry when he recognized her parents in the photos on the office wall.

In fact, now that she was less rattled and more able to sanely consider their whole conversation, he'd seemed angry the entire time, although his words were polite enough.

She rubbed her right temple where a headache was growing steadily stronger.

"What do you think, Allison?"

Yanked back to the present, Allison focused on a line chart propped on the easel standing at the far end of the long table. The accountant was pointing to the third column and looking at her expectantly.

"I'm sorry, I didn't catch that. Could you go over it again, please?"

The accountant barely managed to conceal his annoyance, but he moved to the first column and began to repeat his explanation.

Allison determinedly focused on his words, refusing to let Jorge, the baby and what she was going to do about both of those impossible subjects, distract her again.

Later that night, despite an exhausting day that required working late to complete legal research, Jorge lay awake, his hands stacked beneath his head, staring at the ceiling above his rumpled bed.

The scene with Allison kept playing over and over in his mind. The intuition that made him so formidable in the courtroom was telling him that something about their conversation wasn't quite right, but he couldn't put his finger on exactly what was wrong.

It could simply be that the laughing Allison in the black lace evening gown seemed to be the complete opposite of the sober Allison in the conservative suit. He wondered briefly if there was any likelihood that she might have a twin, but quickly discounted the possibility. His body recognized hers; she smelled the same; she felt the same when he took her hand in his. No, the passionate woman in his bed that night and the wary, reserved woman he'd seen today were definitely the same woman.

But why had this Allison felt the need to hide the other Allison? What had caused the wariness and fear in her amber eyes?

Angry though she'd made him, he was determined to find answers to his questions.

She may not expect anything from me, he thought grimly, but I damn sure expect something from her.

He knew part of what he wanted from her was another night in her bed. If there was anything else driving his intense interest in the beautiful redhead, he refused to admit it. His work schedule would keep him out of town for the next few days, but when he returned, he planned to change her mind. He fell asleep plotting a campaign to woo the elusive Allison.

Across town Allison was having her own difficulty sleeping. She'd had to force the words out when she told Jorge that she didn't want anything more from him. Every instinct was screaming no as she'd said the words.

What would he say, what would he do, if he knew that their one incredible night of making love had created a child? Would he be pleased that he was going to be a father?

Not likely, she admitted bleakly. It was far more likely that he'd be annoyed and irritated that his fast-paced lifestyle was being interrupted by her pregnancy. Or worse yet, what if he demanded that she get rid of the baby?

Allison knew that she didn't know Jorge well enough to make such an assumption, but she couldn't escape the nagging concern. Like her father, Jorge Perez was a powerful man with a great deal of influence.

He scares me, she admitted. Her hands lay folded over her midsection, and she patted her tummy consolingly. *It's okay, little baby. Mama won't let anything happen to you.*

She drifted off to sleep, unconsciously cradling the tiny new life beneath her palms.

The baby she carried was making its presence felt in a very big way. Her body was increasingly affected by the little one growing within her. After showering on Saturday morning, she realized that she was having difficulty fastening her bra. She twisted and struggled to hook the back closure, then stood in front of the bedroom mirror, naked but for the powder-blue lace bra, and frowned at her reflection.

Her bra was too small. She turned sideways to see the hooks straining the elastic fabric below her shoulderblades, then faced the mirror again. Her breasts were fuller, overflowing the bra cups, the nipples sensitive to the chafe of silk and lace.

She turned sideways once again and smoothed a hand over her still-flat abdomen.

At least I'm not showing here.

With quick decision, she put aside her earlier plans to spend the morning doing homework for her Tuesday-night class in domestic law. Instead, she pulled on panties, jeans, a loose-knit top, and sat on the edge of the bed to tug on her boots. Then she grabbed her purse and jacket and left the apartment for a much-needed shopping trip. Fortunately for Allison, Zoe was out of town for two weeks, visiting her parents and married sister in upstate New York, otherwise, she would undoubtedly have noticed Allison's preoccupation and demanded to know what was bothering her. Allison knew that she couldn't fool Zoe for long and doubted that she'd even try. Her friend had the skills of a trained inquisitor.

At work on Monday, Allison decided wearing comfortable bras was an enormous help, but she was struggling with yet another side effect of her pregnancy. The urge to take a nap after lunch was overwhelming. She was so tired that she was tempted to lock her door, curl up on the comfortable carpet and fall asleep. And her normal, average appetite was suddenly enormous. Instead of downing a cup of yogurt and a banana while working at her desk, she found herself ordering in take-out from the Thai restaurant down the block. Not just one entrée, but two or three, with a side order of sticky rice.

She'd always loved Thai food, but this was ridiculous.

If she kept this up, she was going to gain a hundred pounds before the baby was born she thought, eyeing the four cardboard containers lined up on her desk. Not to mention the fact that somebody was going to start wondering why she was suddenly eating so much food. She frowned and popped a bite of chicken with peanut sauce into her mouth, chewing slowly as she contemplated the possibility. Leah gave her a very funny look when the delivery boy arrived with the food. Maybe Leah suspected?

If anyone might guess, it was Leah. Allison vividly remembered shuddering as she watched the petite receptionist spread sour pickles with peanut butter before eating them. She'd been genuinely concerned about what the odd combination might do to Leah's stomach before the receptionist had reassured her that her obstetrician had told her that strange cravings were perfectly normal during a pregnancy.

Allison sat bolt upright in her chair, her hand holding chopsticks clutching sticky rice, bean sprouts and shrimp, frozen in midair.

Obstetrician? Ohmigod. I don't have an obstetrician!

She dropped the chopsticks into one of the containers and pulled open a desk drawer to reach for her phone book.

She flipped through the yellow pages until she reached the physicians section with its listing of specialties, running her forefinger down the listings until she reached the name she was searching for. She circled the doctor's name and phone number, then dialed.

Several moments later she had an appointment. Unfortunately, it was a whole week away and she'd really wanted to have an exam sooner. The prenatal care book that she'd bought over the weekend stressed the importance of early monitoring by a physician.

And vitamins, she thought. She should be taking vitamins. She glanced at the half-empty containers of Thai food and frowned. Maybe she shouldn't be eating spicy food. She'd read that section of the book tonight.

In the meantime, though, she knew that she could do something about the vitamin issue. She wouldn't have a prescription for prenatal vitamins until after the first visit with her doctor. But the Manhattan Multiples' exam rooms were all stocked with vitamins, it was one of the many benefits provided to clients, so there was no reason she couldn't start taking them immediately.

She'd borrow a bottle. And return it when she got her prescription filled.

Later that afternoon, she visited one of the examination rooms, quickly searched a cabinet, located a bottle of the mega-size vitamins, and tucked it into the white paper bag with the Thai restaurant logo printed prominently on both sides.

She pulled open the door to the hallway and looked out, relieved to find the hall empty. In her haste to exit, she bumped the heavy plastic, bag-covered bottle against the metal trash can just inside the door.

The clattering of the metal can sounded as loud as an explosion to her sensitive ears. Swiftly, she pulled the door shut and hurried off down the hall, barely drawing breath until she was safely back in her office and the bottle of vitamins tucked into the bottom of her purse.

I'm not cut out for all this sneaking around. She blotted the perspiration from her upper lip and tossed the tissue into the wastebasket beneath her desk. She would have made a really incompetent spy.

Allison glanced at the to-do list in her dayplanner, tucked it back into her purse, and dialed the phone. Moments later her yoga class was successfully switched to a prenatal group at an earlier time.

Satisfied that she'd accomplished as much as possible on her pregnancy to-do list, she pulled up the data file for the new security company and spent the next hour modifying the contract to meet the strict requirements Eloise had requested.

At last, satisfied with the wording, she hit the print button and waited for the printer to spit out the clean pages. Then she gathered them into a folder, paper clipped the appropriate signature lines and left her office.

Eloise's office door was partially ajar, and Allison could hear her talking, although she couldn't make out the words. She paused a moment before knocking, but didn't hear a response so, hoping that she wasn't interrupting Eloise and a client, tapped softly on the door panel.

"Yes?"

Eloise's voice was distracted, slightly impatient.

Allison pushed open the door and stepped inside, glancing around the room. Eloise was alone, sitting behind her desk, a pencil tucked behind her ear and a frown on her face.

"Come in, Allison."

"I hope I'm not interrupting." Allison glanced quickly around the room as she crossed the carpeted floor and dropped into one of two elegant chairs facing the desk, but she saw no one other than Eloise. "I thought I heard voices, were you talking to someone?"

Eloise made a face and gestured at her computer screen. "I was ranting at my computer. I'm trying to write an anonymous letter to the editor, protesting the mayor's position on budget cuts, and it isn't going well."

She ran her fingers through her hair, tousling the normally neat locks, and glared at the computer again.

"Is there anything I can do to help?" Allison asked, well aware that Eloise was worried about the mayor's proposed budget cuts and how they would affect the funding for Manhattan Multiples' operating expenses.

"You can read what I've written so far and give me your opinion." Eloise hit the print button, and the machine hummed, then spat out a copy. "Here it is—be honest." She held out the two-page letter.

Silence reigned for the few moments it took for Allison to read the pages. She reread two of the paragraphs before she looked up.

"Well?" Eloise asked.

"I think you've stated the case for keeping budget funding in place for women's and children's programs very well—brilliantly, in fact."

"But...?"

"But a couple of the paragraphs sound a bit too personal."

"Personal?" Eloise bristled, looking decidedly startled.

"Yes. Especially the paragraph accusing the mayor of choosing financial interests over the welfare of children and pregnant women."

"But that's exactly what he's doing!"

"Perhaps." Allison searched for a way to make Eloise understand her view.

"This is a political issue, not a personal one." Eloise continued adamantly, "Bill Harper is using his position as mayor of New York City to destroy Manhattan Multiples, all in the name of capitalism. It's unconscionable."

"I'm not saying that you're wrong about him, only that the wording in your letter sounds a bit as if you feel that the mayor is attacking you personally." Allison privately thought that Eloise was taking her disagreement with the mayor's position very personally. And that was unlike the levelheaded, business-wise Eloise. In fact, it was unlike Eloise to be so passionately argumentative about any issue.

"Show me which paragraphs."

Allison leaned forward, pointing out the paragraphs on her copy. Eloise frowned and turned back to her computer screen, quickly scrolling down to the offending sentences.

"Hmm." She sighed. "I'll have to work on it some more. I was really hoping to send it off this afternoon."

"Would you like me to take this copy back to

my office and do some editing, perhaps come up with some possible rewording of the paragraphs?''

"Thanks, Allison, that would be very helpful."

Allison smiled at the look of relief Eloise gave her. She stood, placing the file containing the security contracts on top of the in-box on the corner of the desk. "I'll take this copy with me—and here are the contracts for the installation of the additional alarms. I've paper-clipped the pages that need your signature."

"Thanks, Allison, you're a treasure."

"No problem. I'll e-mail you with input on the letter."

"Great!"

As Allison left the office, Eloise was already refocused on her computer screen, muttering to herself as she typed.

While Eloise was revising her passionate letter to the editor, across town in the mayor's office, Bill Harper sat alone, staring at a photograph of Eloise. His office was usually chaotic, but a meeting had been canceled at the last minute and in a rare, private moment he had time to close his door, ask his secretary to hold his calls and draw a deep breath. He couldn't help but regret so much about his shared past with Eloise. Their current situation had put them at loggerheads over his need to balance the city's budget and her need for funding of her beloved business.

I wonder if we'll ever be friends again.

He stroked his fingertips over the cool glass separating him from the colored photo. She was as beautiful now as she'd been when he'd first fallen in love with her all those years ago, when they were so young. She'd married another man, but he'd never stopped loving her.

The intercom buzzed, demanding his attention.

Bill sighed, returned the framed photo to its place among the collection on the bookcase near his desk and picked up the phone. His few moments of quiet were over.

If Allison could have seen the mayor as he gazed at the photo of her boss, she would have known instantly that her boss had lied to her. The connection between Mayor Harper and Eloise Vale clearly was deeply personal.

Chapter Three

Allison glanced at the small clock on the stove and blinked.

"Midnight already?" She smothered a yawn as she pushed back her chair and stood to stretch. Bracing her hands against the ache at the small of her back, she arched, twisting right, then left, in an attempt to relieve stiff muscles.

Her prepregnancy habit of going straight from the office to study at the law library on the weeknights that she didn't have class was no longer possible. Instead, she'd taken to coming straight home for a nap and setting her alarm to wake her at 9:00 p.m. Tonight she'd staggered out of bed at nine and microwaved a container of leftover pasta for dinner, eating the meal while jotting down notes for a class on criminal law later in the week. The weariness that dragged at her during the day wouldn't be held off for long, however, and now, three hours later, she was thoroughly exhausted.

She closed her books and left the kitchen for the bathroom, where she brushed her teeth, washed her face, combed out her hair and pulled on loose flannel pajamas. She turned sideways to view her profile in the mirror and smoothed the flannel snugly over her midriff.

Still no little bump. But she knew that her baby wouldn't stay hidden for long.

Her baby. The words still stunned her. And she was no closer to making the necessary big decisions.

Some things she knew without question. She knew that she was fiercely determined to raise her child in the best circumstances possible. Although the effort was exhausting her, she was determined to continue taking classes to earn her law degree. She knew she needed a better income to support her baby than her current salary at Manhattan Multiples.

But she still struggled to come to grips with the impact the little one would inevitably have on her life. And ever since Jorge's visit to her office, she'd wrestled with the question of telling him about the child they'd created. Should she tell him? Could she? Surely he had the right to know, but would he care?

The unanswered questions kept her awake at night, adding to her weariness.

By five o'clock the following evening, Allison was worn-out. When she left the office, the evening held the chill of fall, the sky overcast and threatening rain. Shivering, she huddled deeper into her coat, pulling the collar up under her chin, and ducked her head against the sting of the wind. Much as she longed to hurry home to the warmth of her apartment, she resolutely made her way to the campus lecture hall for her night class. She took a seat in a nearly empty row near the back of the tier of auditorium chairs and warmed her hands by cradling a hot cup of herbal tea. The kiosk outside the quad was doing a brisk business in the cold evening, and fortunately for Allison's cold face and hands, the owners delivered fast service.

"Excuse me."

Allison looked over her shoulder, then half turned when she recognized a woman she'd seen in several other classes.

"Hi."

"Hi. Do you know who's lecturing tonight? I heard that the scheduled speaker had a conflicting engagement and we're getting a sub."

"I haven't a clue," Allison admitted. "To be

honest, I'd totally forgotten that Professor Smythe was out of town this week.''

''Well, whoever it is, I hope they're better than the last sub we had.''

Allison nodded, a wry grin curving her mouth. ''If they're not, I'm out of here.''

''Me, too.'' The other woman nodded emphatically. Her gaze moved past Allison and her eyes widened. ''Whoa, things are looking up.''

Curious, Allison turned to look at the lecture floor below. A tall, broad-shouldered man had his back to them as he shrugged out of his overcoat and tossed it over one end of the heavy oak library table that served as a desk.

He looked familiar. Allison frowned. Too familiar. Glossy, short black hair gleamed under the overhead lights, his gray wool suit coat tailored to fit perfectly across the wide span of his shoulders.

It can't be. Allison stared intently, willing the man to turn around.

When he did, she gasped. She squeezed her eyes shut, then opened them wide. Jorge Perez was still there, opening a leather briefcase and removing a sheaf of notes, glancing around the small hall at the theater seats that were swiftly filling with students.

What was he doing here? She instinctively sank lower in her seat to avoid being seen. Unfortunately, the two seats in front of her were empty, and when she shifted, Jorge's gaze zeroed in on the movement. She froze. She couldn't tell from this distance, but she thought his gaze sharpened for a moment before it moved on.

A surge of heat drove away all the remaining impact of the chilly night outside. Allison felt her fingers tingle. Her throat and cheeks grew warmer, and she tensed, glancing about her for fear that her intense reaction to Jorge was visible. But none of her classmates were paying any attention to her. All of the women were much too busy ogling Jorge while the men appeared preoccupied with studying.

"Nice substitute," the woman seated behind Allison leaned forward to whisper. "I don't think I care if he's a good speaker. Just looking at him for two hours is enough."

Allison managed a weak chuckle and nodded as if in agreement.

Three women moved down the aisle and took the seats next to Allison.

"Hey," the one nearest to Allison murmured to her companions, "Check out the professor."

"Nice," one commented while the other heaved a theatrical sigh and fanned herself.

"Better than nice. Hot, very hot."

"Who is he? And I wonder if he's married?"

"Who cares?" The woman seated next to Allison laughed. "Being married just means that he isn't available. It doesn't mean that we can't window-shop."

Allison gritted her teeth and bit back a scathing comment. She found their remarks seriously annoying, and for a reckless moment, considered telling them so.

Oh, no. She nearly groaned out loud. The sudden knowledge that her annoyance was fueled by jealousy hit her like a blow.

I don't want to feel this. One night in his bed doesn't mean I have a reason to resent other women who find him attractive. He isn't mine.

Unfortunately, knowing that Jorge wasn't connected to her by either affection, promises, or wedding vows didn't stop her from becoming irritated by the other women. She bit her tongue to keep from responding a half-dozen times before Jorge called the class to order and their comments ceased.

In the next hour and a half, Allison took notes almost nonstop. If the female students had first noticed Jorge's handsome face and body, they quickly learned that an incisive mind and formidable intelligence made him far more than a pretty face.

He rarely consulted his notes, pacing back and forth as he lectured, his gaze moving over the audience for the occasional raised hand. He answered each question concisely, ensuring that the student understood his response before he moved on. He didn't however, acknowledge Allison by so much as a smile or the slightest alteration of his expression when his dark gaze moved over her. His glance was impersonal and so lacking in recognition that she felt rebuffed.

By the time he completed his lecture and called for questions, Allison was exhausted. She dropped her pen on top of her notebook, flexing her fingers in an effort to ease the tired muscles as she listened to students' questions and Jorge's responses. After a few moments of hearing him explain points of constitutional law that she felt he'd already thoroughly explored in the lecture, she stifled a yawn. The intense concentration she'd focused on Jorge's lecture had dissipated, leaving her feeling even more tired than usual.

Her eyelids felt as if they were weighted with stones. She hid another yawn, realized that she was nodding, and purposely opened her eyes wide. Within seconds she yawned again, her eyes half-closed. She glanced at her watch, considering stealthily leaving the lecture hall, but just then Jorge looked directly at her. She stiffened, but his gaze hesitated only a moment before it moved on.

She pushed back her cuff and looked at her watch again.

Only twenty more minutes. Surely I can stay awake for another twenty minutes.

She pulled her coat around her shoulders and forced herself to focus on the intense student in the third row and his question regarding the constitutionality of the Miranda ruling.

"Allison. Allison?"

"Mmm?" Someone was calling her name. Allison came awake slowly. It took an amazing effort to lift her heavy lashes and focus.

"Are you all right?"

Jorge bent over her, frowning, his hand on her arm. Allison realized that it was his voice and the gentle shake he'd given her shoulder that had wakened her. Disoriented, she looked away from him and realized that the lecture hall was empty except for the two of them.

Startled, she sat upright, making a quick grab for and missing the notebook and pen that immediately slid off her lap and on to the floor.

"Where is everyone?"

Jorge's dark gaze scanned her face before he bent to pick up her pen and notebook. "Class is over, everyone's gone."

"I fell asleep." She was much too drowsy, total wakefulness a goal she couldn't reach. She knew she shouldn't encourage Jorge to talk with her for fear that she might accidentally make a comment that would lead him to suspect her pregnancy, but her defenses were lowered by exhaustion and the same warm sense of connection flowing between them that she'd felt that night on the terrace.

Jorge smiled, his gaze warming. "Yes, I think you did. Was my lecture that boring?"

He handed her the notebook and pen and she

turned away from him, tucking them into her bag on the adjoining seat.

"Thank you. And no, the lecture was very good. I'm just really tired tonight, didn't get enough sleep last night." She drew a deep breath, fumbling with her coat and avoiding meeting his eyes. "I'd better go." She gathered her bag, scarf and gloves.

Jorge stepped back into the aisle, taking her arm as she rose, then releasing her as she moved past him and started up the aisle to the exit doors.

He reached around her, his much larger body bracketing hers for a brief, heartstopping moment as he turned the latch and shoved open the door. He stood so close that his scent assailed her senses, evoking vivid memories of the night they spent together. The urge to lean forward and bury her face against the strong pulse at his throat to breathe in the smell that was uniquely Jorge was so strong that Allison panicked and jerked quickly away from him, stumbling out into the night. The wind, driving rain before it, swept beneath the roof overhang, catching her breath and chilling her to the bone.

"You're shivering." Jorge raised an umbrella and held it over her, protecting her from the cold rain while his body blocked the wind. "Which way is your car?"

"I don't have a car. I'll catch a taxi at the corner." Allison gestured toward the far end of the block of brick buildings where the street glistened with rain beneath the streetlamps. There wasn't a taxi in sight, she realized with dismay.

Jorge slipped an arm around her shoulders, tucked her close, and, holding the umbrella over them both, walked toward the parking garage. Allison was so tired that she didn't protest when he halted by a forest green Jaguar. He thumbed the control on his key ring, and the car beeped gently, headlights flashing once, twice, in response.

"What are you doing?"

He pulled open the passenger door. "I'm taking you home." He paused, his arm still around her shoulders. "Are you going to argue with me, or are you going to be reasonable?"

Allison knew she should refuse his offer. The more time she spent in his company, the greater the chance that she might accidentally let something slip about her pregnancy. But she was so tired. She glanced outside the garage to the street corner, empty of taxis, and shivered at a gust of cold, wet wind.

"No, I'm not going to argue with you."

"Good." His voice rang with satisfaction.

Jorge helped her into the car, waiting until she was settled before closing the door. The comfortable interior smelled of leather and the brand of men's cologne Allison associated with him. Within seconds he was sliding beneath the wheel, the door shutting with a solid thunk and closing the two of them in together, safely out of the forbidding weather. He twisted the ignition key, and the engine came to life with a throaty purr.

"We'll have warm air in a second," he commented. He half turned in his seat to reach her seat belt, his chest and arms pressing against hers for one breath-stealing moment until his fingers found the belt. He pulled it forward and across her breasts and midriff, his bent head inches from hers, and slotted the buckle into the latch. Then he looked up, his face too close to hers, his eyes enigmatic.

For a moment Allison felt surrounded by him, and she longed to touch him. But then he moved back, breaking the spell. She felt bereft, her body having been denied the contact it craved.

He slipped his own seat belt into place, shifted the car into gear, glanced over his shoulder and pulled smoothly out into the sparse traffic. His gaze flicked over her, and he pushed a button on the dash. Warm air poured out of the vents, heating her cold feet, legs and body.

She sighed in appreciation.

"Better?"

"Much."

He turned on the radio, soft Latin music filling the comfortable interior. A great wave of weariness washed over Allison, and she rested her head against the soft leather seat, eyes half-closed as she watched the familiar streets slip by. The rain drummed a soft tattoo on the roof of the car, and she dozed, lulled by the music of radio and rain.

"Hey, are you falling asleep on me again?" Jorge's voice was half teasing, half concerned. "Are you feeling well? Should I get a doctor?"

Allison smiled sleepily, snuggling deeper into the comfortable soft leather seat. "No, and no. I'm perfectly fine. The books say it's normal to be tired during the first trimester. Exhaustion is just part of being a little bit pregnant."

The moment the word *pregnant* left her lips, Allison realized, too late, what she had done. The silence in the car was electric, tension vibrating, destroying the peaceful atmosphere that had existed only moments before. She stiffened, bracing herself for rejection, and opened her eyes. Jorge's profile was etched against the dark night outside by the soft dashlights inside. Faint though the light was, she could see the taut line of his jaw, lips, nose and brow as he stared at the road ahead.

Jorge was stunned, swamped by a mix of powerful emotions. Joy that he was going to be a father and a fierce desire to claim the fragile redhead fought with anger. Not only had she omitted telling him that she was pregnant with his baby, but she seemed determined to keep him out of her life.

"You're a little bit pregnant?" The words were even, careful, barely a question.

"Yes."

The whispered confirmation sent a shaft of fierce exultation through him. He glanced at her. Her face was turned toward him, her amber eyes wide, shadowed with worry.

"And it's mine."

It wasn't a question. It was a statement of claim. He read the knowledge in her eyes.

He turned his attention back to driving. The following long silence stretched Allison's nerves. Then he swung his car to the curb, expertly wedging it into a narrow parking space.

Allison looked up at the facade of her apartment building, a faint frown of confusion veeing her brows. "How did you know where I live?"

He glanced at her and switched off the engine. "I looked up your address."

He didn't wait for her response. Instead, he shoved open the driver's door and left the car, rounding the hood to open her door and snap open the umbrella. She stepped out on to the curb and he slammed the door, thumbing the lock control as he reached for her bag and took her arm, walking with her up the steps of her building and into the foyer.

"Keys." He lowered the umbrella. Water streamed from the furled material and on to the marble floor, pooling beneath their feet, but neither of them noticed.

She fumbled in her bag. The light over the glass double doors gleamed off the crown of her bent head. When she located her keys and looked up at him, that same light revealed shadows beneath her eyes. She dropped the key ring into his outstretched hand.

He ignored the questions in her eyes and reached around her to unlock the door. His body crowded hers until he pulled the heavy door open and stood back to let her enter the lobby ahead of him.

She turned, opening her mouth to speak.

"I'm coming up."

She stared at him for one silent moment.

"Very well." She spun on her heel, clearly wide awake now, and walked quickly to the stairwell. She didn't look back. Jorge was barely a step behind. He knew he was pushing her, but he didn't care. He was fighting the urge to sweep her into his arms and carry her upstairs.

Allison waited until they entered her apartment and the door closed behind them before she spoke. Her nerves were stretched taut. His reaction to her letting slip the word *pregnancy* in the car had been calm and controlled, but he'd prowled behind her as if he were stalking her after they left the car.

"I'm sure you have questions." She didn't look at him, concentrating on slipping out of her coat.

"Several."

She started, unaware that he'd walked up behind

her. He lifted the coat from her nerveless fingers and tossed it over the back of the sofa, plucked her scarf and gloves from her hands and dropped them on to the coat. Then he shrugged out of his own coat and tossed it over the back of the old wooden rocker next to the sofa.

"You look chilled to the bone."

She wrapped her arms around her midriff and nodded. "I am." Still nervous, she glanced around her at the living room where seating consisted of a small sofa, one overstuffed chair and the wooden rocker holding his coat. "Why don't I make us some tea or coffee?"

"Either is fine with me." He followed her into the small kitchen, catching her elbow and urging her gently into one of the wooden chairs at the small table. "Sit. I'll make it." He eyed her critically, lifting a brow in inquiry. "I'm guessing you'd prefer tea?"

"Yes—but I have coffee if you'd rather..."

"No, tea's fine."

He picked up the teakettle from the range and held it under the tap, the sound of water rushing into the kettle the only sound in the quiet room. Finished, he returned the kettle to the stove and switched on the burner.

Allison sat, frantically trying to organize her jumbled thoughts, while he opened cabinet doors and took out mugs and tea.

"We'll get married, of course. As soon as possible. What are you doing this weekend?"

Allison was stunned. She opened her mouth to speak, but no words came out.

He turned, leaned his hips against the cabinets behind him, crossed his arms over his chest and eyed her, waiting for a response.

She could only stare at him, caught completely off guard.

A rueful smile lit his eyes.

"I think you're the first woman I've ever actually struck speechless, Allison."

"I wasn't expecting…" She paused, helpless. A small ember of hope glowed deep within her. Did he care for her? Had that one magical night they'd spent together meant something important to him, as much as it had to her?

"A baby? Neither was I." His gaze was enigmatic, hooded. "But you didn't get pregnant alone, Allison, and I won't let you face raising a child alone, either. This baby belongs to both of us, needs both of us. And the only practical solution for us to share him, or her, is to marry."

Allison's heart fell, his words grinding out the small spark of hope. "I…" She paused, swallowing past the lump of emotion that choked off her words. "I don't know what to say."

"Say yes."

She stared at him, yearning for something more

than the calm, reasonable words that spelled out a future dictated by practicality but without the heady joy of love. "I need time to think," she said, finally. "It never occurred to me that you would consider marriage for the sake of the baby."

He scowled. "What did you think? That I'm the kind of guy who'd bail and leave you to cope with the consequences?"

"I didn't know what to think." She gestured helplessly. "Most men would."

A muscle ticked along his jawline. "I'm not most men," he said tightly.

She knew that, she realized with sudden clarity. If he had been like most men, this pregnancy would never have happened. She would never have gone to bed with him that night.

"I'm sorry," she said quietly. "I shouldn't have made assumptions about how you'd react."

"No, you shouldn't have." The stern lines of his features eased, softening as he searched her face. "Say yes, Allison. After we marry, we'll have a lifetime to learn to know each other. No more assumptions."

Allison's mind whirled with a thousand questions and worries.

"You don't have to give me an answer tonight." Jorge reached behind him and switched off the teakettle. "You look like you're about to fall asleep sitting in that chair."

With two long strides, he crossed the tiny kitchen and bent, slipping an arm beneath Allison's knees and the other around her waist.

He moved so quickly that she barely had time to draw a startled gasp before he swung her up into his arms and left the kitchen.

"What are you doing?" She wasn't immune to the heat of his body, the strength of his arms that held her, the scent of his aftershave. She wanted to be. But she wasn't. Memories of the last time he'd held her, without layers of clothing between them, flooded her with Technicolor images.

"Taking you to bed." He looked down at her, wry amusement underlying the heat in his eyes. "Alone. I'll tuck you in and leave. You look too tired to give me an answer tonight. I can wait— until tomorrow."

Before Allison could answer him, he swung her to her feet in the bedroom and left her standing, indecisive, while he switched on the lamp and turned down the bed with quick, efficient movements.

He turned, walked toward her, and the intimacy of the lamplit bedroom sent alarm bells jangling along Allison's already fraught nerves.

He stopped in front of her, his expression neutral. "I'm going back to the kitchen to warm a mug of milk for you." She grimaced and he smiled. "When I get back, you'll have your nightgown on and be ready to drink the milk and go to sleep, agreed?"

"I don't wear a nightgown. I wear pajamas."

His smile deepened with affection, warming Allison and soothing her nerves.

"Okay," he said reasonably. "Then put on your pajamas and get ready for bed."

He tapped his forefinger gently against the tip of her nose, winked, and left the room.

Allison was exhausted and knew she should be relieved that he wasn't exerting the full force of his irresistible sexual appeal. But she couldn't deny that on some level she was annoyed that he was treating her like a five-year-old favorite niece.

Disgruntled, she pulled flannel pajamas from the chest of drawers against the far wall and locked herself into the minuscule bathroom across the even tinier hallway. Face scrubbed, teeth brushed, dressed in oversize blue pajamas patterned with little white flower sprigs, she climbed into bed and tucked the pillows behind her. She barely finished when Jorge returned.

He paused abruptly in the doorway, his gaze running swiftly over her face and the blanket-covered shape of her in the bed. For a moment Allison felt swift heat spin between them, but then his eyes shuttered, banking the flare of sexual awareness. He left the doorway and walked to the bed, handing her a gently steaming mug.

She frowned, first at the warm milk, then at him.

"Think of it as medicine." He grinned at her. "It's good for the baby and it's good for you. It'll help you sleep."

"I hate warm milk," she commented, sipping.

"Can't say that I blame you." He leaned over the bed, tucking the blanket closer against her waist. Then he planted the flat of his palms against the blankets on either side of her and looked at her. Their faces were barely a foot apart.

He had the most beautiful eyes. Allison stared at him, drinking in the male beauty in the angles and planes of cheekbones, jaw, the curve of his ear and eyebrows, and the absurdly thick sweep of black eyelashes surrounding dark-chocolate eyes. The lamplight gleamed, highlighting the golden sheen of his skin. Allison badly wanted to lean forward and bury her face against the warm curve of his throat, but she gripped the mug until her fingers ached and forced herself to remain where she was.

"Promise me you'll finish the milk?" His voice was a deep murmur, rumbling softly in the quiet, dimly lit room.

"I'll finish the milk," she said with solemn politeness. "But I won't like it."

His lips quirked in a heartstopping smile, the long sweep of his lashes half concealing the gleam of amusement in his eyes.

"Okay. You don't have to like it, just as long as you finish it and it helps you to sleep."

Allison eyed him wryly. "I didn't have any difficulty falling asleep earlier tonight, what makes you think I'll need help?"

"Good point." His gaze dropped to her mouth, then lifted slowly to meet hers once again.

Allison caught her breath at the heat in his eyes, visible for only a moment before his lashes lowered, hiding his expression from her.

Abruptly he shoved upright, standing beside her bed. "I'll pick you up for lunch tomorrow. I hope you'll have an answer for me by then."

"That's not very long to think about getting engaged."

"Not engaged. Married. And I wish I could give you longer, but we've waited long enough as it is. I want your name changed before the baby gets here."

"I can't promise you that I'll have an answer for you by tomorrow," she said stubbornly.

"All right. Promise me that you'll consider it?"

"Yes."

"Good." He bent over the bed, the warm brush of his lips against her brow, chaste though the kiss was, was somehow comforting. "I'll pick you up at your office tomorrow at noon for lunch."

He turned at the door and glanced back at her. "Good night, Allison."

"Good night," she whispered.

Allison sat motionless, listening to the sound of his footsteps as he crossed the living room, the click of the dead bolt being released, the snick of the door opening and closing, then silence.

He wanted to get married. But only because he wanted the baby.

She forced herself to sip the still-warm milk.

She fiercely wanted this baby, and she knew that she would find a way to do whatever was necessary to care for her child, but there was no question that the joy and worry of raising him or her would be infinitely easier if she could share the experience with the baby's father.

She was still stunned that he wanted to be an involved father.

She didn't have to marry, she reminded herself. She could always ask her parents for financial help should she ever need it.

She rejected the idea as soon as it occurred. She knew she couldn't bring herself to actively involve her parents in her child's life. The high-powered couple were likely to take over and try to control both her and her baby's life. Allison knew she didn't want her baby to endure the fishbowl life her parents loved and that she herself had struggled with as a child. She was determined to shelter her little one against the stress and demands of fame.

Can I marry Jorge, knowing that he doesn't love

me? But I don't love him, either, she thought. How could she? She hardly knew him beyond the fact that he was an amazing lover. Surely loving someone took longer than one magical, passion-filled night? A part of her scoffed at the analysis, but she determinedly ignored the small voice.

And then, she thought, there's the question of my job. She wasn't quite ready to tell Eloise about her pregnancy, especially since her boss had been grumbling lightly about one of the nurses being pregnant and the need to plan for a replacement during her maternity leave.

She finished her milk and set the empty mug on the nightstand. Sighing, she pushed her fingers through her hair, tucking it behind her ears before she wrapped her arms around her legs and rested her chin on her knees.

So many things to consider, she thought. And she couldn't allow her feelings alone to make her decision. Didn't Jorge deserve to be a full-time father to their child? Didn't the baby deserve to have his or her father as a constant presence in their life?

She had no idea how living with Jorge as man and wife would work out. In fact, she couldn't even conceive of the concept without getting huge butterflies in her stomach. But she knew that she owed it to both of them, and to their unborn child, to consider the prospect.

The butterflies fluttered and she pressed a hand to her still-flat tummy.

He scares me to death, she acknowledged. She suspected that she could easily fall in love with him, and if she did, would he break her heart if he didn't love her back?

Her stomach roiled. It was unlike her to be so indecisive. She was frightened of her feelings for Jorge and the possibility that they might grow stronger. She was equally terrified by the changes she felt in her body and the knowledge that the baby's impact on her body would soon escalate.

Frustrated by her inability to focus and arrive at a clear, considered decision, Allison turned out the lamp and pulled the blankets up to her chin. Determinedly she closed her eyes and began to recite the lyrics to her favorite Bob Dylan song, while she purposely drew slow, controlled, rhythmic breaths.

She was so exhausted that she didn't complete the second verse after the bridge before she was fast asleep.

Jorge drove home in a state of elation edged with worry. His first instinct had been to carry Allison off to bed and keep her there until she agreed to marry him. The sexual attraction that pulsed between them on that long-ago night was still there, as strong as ever. But he'd purposely banked the heat between them because her amber eyes held a fear and wariness that he didn't understand. Until he knew why she was so wary, he couldn't chance giving her cause to refuse him. Until she wore his ring on her finger, had given her promise in front of a justice of the peace and he legally owned the right to claim her, he'd do his damnedest to keep his hormones in check. Until he learned why she was afraid, he would try to be patient.

And patience wasn't something he was good at, he reflected. Not when it came to wanting Allison Baker.

Chapter Four

The following morning dawned bright and clear, the rainstorm blowing itself out during the night and giving way to crisp air, cold temperature and blue skies. The radio alarm woke Allison at her usual early hour, and after a full night's sleep she was relieved to discover that the morning brought clearer insight.

She was still afraid that marrying Jorge would endanger her heart, but she was convinced that marriage was the best thing for their child.

Tossing back the blankets, she left the bed to shower and dress for the day. Two hours later she was at her desk, absorbed in compiling statistics for

Eloise's latest project. She purposely turned off the automatic clock on her computer and removed her watch, tucking it into her purse. If she didn't, she was sure that she'd spend all morning agonizing over her approaching lunch date with Jorge.

Fortunately for her state of mind, her plan worked. After several false starts, she lost track of time until Leah interrupted her several hours later.

"Allison?"

She looked up. "Hi, Leah, what is it?"

"That gorgeous guy is back again. He says you're expecting him?"

Allison's heart jumped, but she managed to nod calmly. "Yes, we have a lunch date. Would you tell him that I'll be right out?"

"Sure."

Leah disappeared and Allison opened her bottom desk drawer, took out her purse and found her lipstick case. The little mirror reflected a calm, cool exterior that revealed none of the nervousness that had little butterflies fluttering their wings in her midsection. Reassured, she slicked pink color over her lips, ran a brush through already neat hair, slipped into her coat and left her office.

When she walked into the reception area, she found Jorge across the room, his back to her, studying an original watercolor painted by one of the clinic's clients.

Her heart did the fast, trip-hammer beat that she

was growing accustomed to feeling every time she saw him. Determined to ignore it, she pinned a smile on her face and walked toward him.

"Hello, Jorge."

He looked over his shoulder, his gaze meeting hers, and her heart stuttered, then thudded heavily in response to his heavy-lidded, swift appraisal.

"Hello, Allison." His gaze flicked over her coat and purse. "Ready to leave?"

"Yes."

"Good." He took her elbow and ushered her out of the office. Even through the layers of coats that separated them, Allison's rebellious body reacted with heat and a tingling awareness that radiated from the loose clasp of his hand on her arm.

The restaurant he chose for their lunch was only a short block from her office, the furnishings elegant, the wine list exclusive, the privacy optimal.

"Do you eat here often?" she asked, glancing around the softly lit room with its huge potted palms discreetly screening tables.

"On occasion." Jorge's gaze followed hers, then returned to her menu, forgotten on the table in front of her. "Have you decided?"

"Oh, no, I haven't." She scanned the entrées and looked up at him. "Do you have a favorite? Can you suggest something?"

"Would you like me to order for you?" he asked.

"Yes, please." Allison didn't really care what he ordered because she doubted that she'd be able to taste the food. She was far too tense to care, although the growing baby inside her required that she eat at regular intervals.

He gave the waiter their order, green salads and grilled fish with sautéed mixed vegetables. Plain food without rich sauces that might upset her fragile stomach, Allison noted with relief.

"And I'll have coffee." He handed the menu to the waiter and glanced at Allison, lifting a brow in inquiry. "What would you like to drink? Tea? Milk?"

His gaze held hers, and Allison had a swift mental image of him leaning over her in the lamplit bedroom, heat flickering in the depths of his eyes when he'd handed her the glass of warm milk. She should never have allowed him into her bedroom last night, she thought. And she wouldn't have if she hadn't been so tired, her defenses weakened. Despite the fact that he'd been an absolute gentleman, the air had been charged with sexual tension. Just as it was now.

"I'll have herbal tea, thank you," she told the waiter.

Neither of them spoke until the young man left. Then Jorge settled back in his chair and eyed her, turning his glass in slow circles on the tabletop. "Have you made a decision?"

"Yes, I have." Calm though she was on the outside, Allison was shaking with nerves on the inside. Amazingly enough, her hand didn't tremble when she picked up her glass and took a sip of water. Carefully, she returned the stemmed crystal to the snowy tablecloth and met his gaze.

"I've thought about what you said last night—" she paused, searching for words.

"And?" he prompted.

His fingers stilled on the stem of his water glass, and Allison realized that his indolent posture was a sham. Beneath the outward appearance of mild interest, his muscles were taut, his jawline tense.

I'm not the only one unsure of this situation, she thought.

The insight calmed her nerves. She drew a deep breath and met his gaze.

"And I agree. Our baby should have both parents in her life full-time. I think we should get married." Fierce emotion flared in his eyes, and his grip tightened on the glass with punishing force. "For the sake of the baby," she added hastily.

Jorge's eyes narrowed, his expression shuttered. "Of course," he murmured. "For the baby." For one long moment he was silent, his gaze fastened on hers. Then he looked away, lifted his glass and drank, the strong column of his throat moving rhythmically as he swallowed. When he set down the glass and looked back at her, his gaze was unreadable. "I think we should get married as soon as possible. Do you have any preferences as to how or where?"

"No, I…" The waiter returned with their food, interrupting Allison. She didn't respond to his question until they were alone once again. "I suppose being married sooner rather than later is best."

"I think so," he commented. "Do you want to make the arrangements or shall I?"

"I could do it." She lifted her shoulders in a helpless shrug. "Although I have no idea what's necessary in New York State."

"I can have my secretary find out, if you'd like."

"That would be great. It's not that I don't want to," she said hastily. "But I have a huge exam in contract law this week and what with my workload at Manhattan Multiples and studying for the test, I'm afraid I won't have time to track down the information we need."

"Don't worry about it." He picked up his fork. "I'll have Laurie research the details and make the arrangements. All you have to do is give me a list of any guests you want invited and show up on the right date. And I'll pick you up, so you don't even have to worry about that."

She looked at him, a wry smile curving her mouth. "I have absolutely nothing to wear. Would you mind if I appeared wearing a sweatshirt and jeans?"

His eyes went hot. "Wear the dress you wore the night we met."

Heat singed her cheeks and throat. "I can't," she whispered. "It's an evening gown, not a wedding dress."

"I don't care." His gaze flicked over her, halted by the table that blocked his view, before moving back upward, lingering on the curve of her breasts, nearly hidden beneath the tailored black suit and white linen blouse. "Wear jeans or nothing at all. Just as long as you're there and say 'I do,' I really don't care what you wear."

"Well, I do," she insisted, refusing to evade his eyes and the undeniable sexual intent in his gaze and words. "I'm not getting married in jeans."

"Fine. I'll get you a dress."

"You will not! I'll buy my own wedding dress."

"Allison," he said softly, steel running beneath the gentle tones. "You don't have to do this alone. You said yourself that your schedule is crazy this coming week. I can make the arrangements, find a dress, reserve the judge. You can focus on studying."

Torn, she bit her lip and considered his words.

"Are you always this stubborn when someone offers to help you?" His deep voice was laced with amusement. Startled, Allison realized that she'd been frowning fiercely at her glass and glanced up to find him watching her, a half smile curving his mouth.

"I'm not sure. The subject doesn't come up that often."

His gaze darkened. "It will from now on."

"Yes, I know." She wouldn't be alone anymore. It was a startling concept and one she could barely grasp. She'd been a solitary child on the fringes of her parents' busy life, and since moving to New York after school, she'd been consumed with work and law classes. Except for Zoe, she'd never really allowed herself to rely on anyone.

"Good. Don't worry about the wedding arrangements or the dress. I'll handle it." He gestured to her plate. "Eat while the food's hot. I'm guessing the baby likes his food warm, and maybe you do, too?"

She laughed. "Yes. I think it's safe to say that we both do." She focused on her still-steaming plate with its cedar-grilled salmon flanked by a sautéed mix of green zucchini, sweet yellow and red bell peppers and fat brown mushrooms and abruptly realized that she was hungry. Very hungry, now that the issue of the wedding was resolved and the butterflies had stopped batting their wings about in her stomach.

It wasn't until her plate was half-empty that she realized Jorge hadn't said a word in several minutes.

She looked up and found him watching her, a slightly bemused look on his face.

"What?" She put down her fork.

"Don't stop eating." He leaned across the table, picked up her fork and tucked it back into her hand. "I can't tell you what a relief it is to see a woman actually enjoy food, instead of nibbling at salad and complaining about the calories."

"I don't have to worry about calories, as a rule. But since becoming pregnant, I'm afraid I'll have to, and soon." Self-conscious, Allison tucked her hair behind her ear.

"Are you gaining weight from the baby already? Isn't it too early?"

"I don't know that I can blame my extra six pounds on the baby, it's just that I suddenly have an enormous appetite." She smiled at him. "If I keep eating like this, I'll be as big as an elephant by the time she arrives."

"I notice you keep calling the baby 'she,'" he commented, his gaze indulgent as she resumed eating. "Do you know for sure that it's a girl?"

Allison shook her head. "No, it's too soon to have an ultrasound to determine the sex." She narrowed her eyes at him. "I notice you keep referring to the baby as 'he.' Do you want a boy?"

He shrugged. "I don't care one way or the other, just as long as both of you are healthy."

Allison was immeasurably reassured by his comment. She knew that it was the baby's health that was most important to him, but that he included her in his concern made her feel cherished.

Jorge returned Allison to her office after lunch and took the long route back to his own. He wasn't ready to face his colleagues; he needed time to consider the changes in his life that Allison's agreement to marriage would mean. He strode away from her building, welcoming the anonymity of the busy city sidewalks.

Freed from the need to control his reaction, the relief and fierce satisfaction that he'd felt when Allison had told him that she agreed to marry him, returned full force. He didn't question the compulsion he felt to bind her to him by every means possible, including marriage. Far from being disappointed that she was pregnant, he was relieved that he had a legitimate reason to demand a place in her life. He knew that she responded to him on a very basic level; she couldn't hide her body's reaction to him, any more than he could control his to her. But there was no avoiding the fact that he read fear and wariness in her eyes whenever he moved close, either physically or emotionally. The difference between the Allison who had spent the night with him and the Allison he'd just spent the past hour with at the restaurant was puzzling.

He frowned, crammed his hands in his coat pockets and walked faster. The unbuttoned topcoat flew open, but he didn't notice the brisk breeze.

He'd heard that pregnancy could make a woman weepy and more emotional. But he didn't remember anyone ever telling him that their wife suddenly became afraid of them.

He wanted the woman he'd spent the night with in his life and in his bed. He wanted to hold her and tell her that everything would be fine, that marriage and a baby would work out for the two of them. But every time he was with her, the look in her eyes backed him away. He had no idea why she would be afraid of him, but he was determined to find out her reasons and do whatever was necessary to erase her wariness.

He had to, for unless he found a way to reassure her that she and their baby were safe with him, their marriage would turn into a nightmare for both of them.

I can do this. Determination firmed his chin. They'd get married as soon as he could make the arrangements, and afterward, when they were living together, he'd have time and opportunity to convince her.

He reached his office and punched the intercom for his secretary as he was shrugging out of his coat.

"Laurie? Will you come in, please?"

He tossed his coat over a chair back, dropped

into his desk chair and was thumbing through his calendar when his secretary entered the office.

He glanced up and waved her to a seat opposite the desk, frowning at the notes jotted on his calendar.

"I need to have my calendar cleared for a week, or at least a long weekend, starting the day of my wedding."

Nearly sixty years old and unflappable in any emergency, Laurie McPherson had worked for Jorge for five years and never once had reacted to news of any sort with less than professional, calm efficiency. So when her jaw dropped in shock and she gasped, it startled him.

"Laurie? What's wrong?"

"What's wrong?" She stared at him. "You're getting married? I didn't even know you were dating anyone. You haven't said a word."

Jorge smiled slowly, delighted at her look of shock. "You mean I've surprised you? I didn't know that was possible."

"Hmph." She shifted in her chair and cleared her throat. "You'll have to admit, marriage isn't something you've ever mentioned."

"You're right. I haven't." He hadn't even considered marriage since his canceled engagement to Celeste. And their engagement hadn't generated a powerful interest in marriage; indeed, he'd been so busy at work that he'd listened only halfheartedly to her plans. He hadn't cared how far off the wedding date was. But with Allison, he realized, he wanted his ring on her finger as soon as he could arrange the ceremony. He looked at his calendar again. "I told Allison that I'd take care of the license, an appointment with the judge, her dress and whatever else needs to be done. Can you find out what I need to do to get a marriage license and if there's a waiting period before we can actually have the ceremony?"

"Sure." She jotted notes on her notepad. "Have you picked a date for the wedding?"

"Just as soon as we can get arrangements finalized. This weekend, if possible, next week at the latest."

To her credit, Laurie didn't bat an eyelash at the time line. "Very well. What judge would you like to have officiate at the ceremony?"

"Judge Maddock."

"And the wedding dress for the bride? What size, style—traditional or modern—color?"

Jorge had a swift mental image of Allison, her creamy skin soft and lush against black lace, auburn hair slipping through his fingers like liquid fire.

But she'd told him that she didn't want to wear the evening gown he'd first seen her in, and it was black.

"Not stark white. Can you find a dress the color

of pale butter? With lace, lots of lace. And a straight skirt, slit up the sides.''

Laurie's pen poised over the paper, her eyebrows lifting. "Do you have a picture of the dress you want for her?"

"No. But it had a low neckline that was sort of off the shoulder." Jorge had no clue what the proper name for Allison's black lace ballgown would be, he just knew he wanted to see her say "I do" in that dress. And if she didn't want to wear that specific dress, then he'd find the closest thing possible.

"Hmm. I'll see if I can find some possible choices for you to look at. What size?"

Jorge's palms itched. He knew the shape and feel of Allison, and could make a guess at what her measurements had been the night she'd shared his bed, but what changes had the baby made? Were her breasts bigger? Her waist a bit less slim?

"I don't know. I'll find out and get back to you."

"All right." Laurie glanced at her notes. "Do you want reservations in town, or are you going away for the honeymoon?"

"Away." He didn't have a clue where, but he knew that he wanted Allison to himself, far enough away from New York City to prevent any interruptions from work.

"Do you want me to make reservations?"

"No." With a sudden flash of inspiration, Jorge

knew where he wanted to go. Ross had a cabin in upstate New York. Picturesque and located in the woods, with a stream running outside the back door and a friendly small town within walking distance, it would be the perfect getaway. "No, I'll do that."

"Okay. If you want this arranged by next week, I'd better get busy." She rose and walked quickly to the door, pausing on the threshold to look back at Jorge. "The research department dropped off the material you requested on search-and-seizure issues in the Kinsey murder. It's in the blue folder in your in-box."

"Thanks." Jorge returned his calendar to the corner of his desk and retrieved the blue file. Within moments he was absorbed in the latest stage of trial preparation for the prominent New York City businessman charged with murdering his high-profile partner.

Allison left her office that evening to find that clouds once again obscured the sun, and cold raindrops spattered the people crowding the sidewalk.

She sighed, tugged her collar higher around her neck and hesitated, reluctant to face the wet, chilly weather. Just as she was about to step out from beneath the shelter of the building's metal awning, a hand closed over the curve of her shoulder.

Startled, she spun about, her eyes widening with surprise.

"Jorge. What are you doing here?"

"Giving you a ride home." He nodded toward the curb, where the green Jaguar sat wedged between a van and a taxi. "Or to campus, if you're going to class."

"No. I'm going home."

He snapped open an umbrella and raised it over her head. "Home it is."

His hand on her waist, he urged her toward the car, shielding her with the umbrella as she ducked her head and slipped into the passenger seat.

The interior of the car was blessedly warm. Allison lowered her coat collar and tugged off her gloves.

Jorge pulled open the door and slid into the driver's seat, closing the door quickly behind him.

"Nasty weather," he muttered, turning to toss the wet, folded umbrella on to the floor in the back.

"Yes, it is," she murmured, shifting to fasten her seat belt.

He turned the key in the ignition and a stream of warm air heated Allison's bare legs beneath the hem of her coat.

"Okay?"

"Lovely." She smiled at him, touched by his thoughtfulness in saving her from the wet, chilly, late-afternoon commute to her apartment.

His eyes darkened, his gaze shifted to her mouth.

Then, without comment, he turned his attention to pulling into traffic.

"I'm surprised that you keep a car in the city," she commented as they inched forward in the heavy stream of cars.

He shrugged. "I don't use it often, usually only on weekends. I catch taxis or hire a car and driver during the week. But I had to drive to Connecticut for a case I'm handling and returned to town with barely enough time to make class last night." He glanced at her, then returned his gaze to the windshield. "What's on your schedule for tonight?"

"Studying and sleeping. Not necessarily in that order."

His gaze flicked over her assessingly. "Maybe sleep first?"

"Maybe." Allison couldn't stifle a yawn. "Probably."

"Then I'll drop you at your apartment and head home." He glanced at her, then back at traffic once again. "There's a possibility that we can have an appointment with a judge for a civil ceremony sometime next week."

Allison's eyes widened. "So soon?"

"I don't see any point in waiting. We agreed that sooner was better than later, didn't we?"

"Yes." She bit her lip, mentally counting days. Barely a week. Her stomach tightened with nerves. "Is there anything we need to do before then?"

"Just pick up the license, and we can do that on our lunch hour tomorrow, if that fits with your schedule."

"Yes, of course." Tension skittered over her skin, tightening her fingers around her gloves.

"And I need to know your measurements."

Her head jerked around, her startled gaze meeting his briefly before he focused on the heavy traffic around them.

"For your dress." His voice lowered, a faint huskiness running below the deep tones, "I could have guessed, but I thought carrying the baby might have made changes and altered your dress size."

Allison felt heat flood her cheeks. She thought about the new bras she'd bought and how much more comfortable they were, frantically wondering if she looked obviously bigger. Sure, her suits were a trifle more snug, but they still fit. Then she remembered she'd told him earlier at lunch that she'd gained six pounds. "I've gained weight but not enough to change my dress size." Yet, she thought. She told him the size she currently wore and he nodded without comment.

"Have you made a list of people you want to invite?"

"It's a very short list, just one person, actually." She'd already decided not to tell anyone at work until after the ceremony. She hoped that presenting them with a fait accompli would cause fewer questions than a pending wedding, although she knew that Eloise would want to know everything about her new husband. She planned to ask Zoe to be her maid of honor over the weekend, just as soon as Zoe returned from visiting her parents upstate.

"Would you like my secretary to contact them, or do you want to do it?"

"I'll ask Zoe." Allison caught the quick, questioning glance he shot her. "Zoe Armbruster. She has the apartment directly across the hall from mine."

"Ah, I think that covers all the questions I need answered immediately."

Allison's eyes drifted closed. She woke as Jorge slowed and nosed the car into the curb. Glancing out the window, she realized that he'd parked in the no-parking, loading zone in front of her apartment building. She unbuckled her seat belt and restrained a shiver at the thought of the chill air between the warm car and the building's entry hall.

Jorge switched off the engine. The resulting silence in the comfortable leather interior of the Jag was suddenly very intimate.

"Do you have any questions about the arrangements for the wedding?" he asked, releasing his seat belt and half turning to face her.

"No, not that I can think of."

"I know this isn't going to be the wedding every girl dreams of," he said gravely, holding her gaze with his. "But if there's anything you want, anything I can accomplish in a week, you'll have it. Just tell me what it is."

Allison fought the urge to cry and only partially succeeded, her voice thick with unshed tears, "That's so sweet of you, Jorge."

"It's not sweet," he growled. "I'm not sweet."

Streaks of color marked his cheekbones, and Allison realized that he was embarrassed. She laughed softly, the low sound made husky by the lump in her throat, and without thought, lifted a hand to cup his cheek. "Maybe not, but I think it's very kind of you to consider my feelings."

His eyes darkened. He covered her hand with his, and she could feel the faint roughness of his razor stubble.

"I'll always consider your feelings, Allison. I want you to be happy."

She could feel the tears trembling on her lashes spill over and trickle slowly down her cheeks.

"I want you to be happy, too, Jorge." *And I'm desperately afraid that I'm ruining your life.*

"Hey," he murmured. His hand left hers to cup her face, his thumb smoothing away the dampness from her cheek. "Don't cry." With easy strength he lifted her, cradling her on his lap, one arm across her back and waist. His fingers returned to wipe away the last of her tears. "We'll be fine, sweetheart. You, me and the baby. Don't worry."

His words brought fresh tears. Allison wanted to ask him how he could be so sure, but his thumb brushed the dampness on her cheeks, then stroked across her bottom lip, and the question was forgotten under the flood of heat that shook her. His gaze lowered, fastened intently on the slow, dragging movements of his thumb against her mouth.

The heat turned into a furnace, burning away the caution that ruled her. Allison's heart shuddered. Jorge's lashes lifted as his gaze left her mouth and met hers. She caught her breath at the raw emotion in the depths of his eyes before his arms tightened. He crushed her closer, his head lowering, and his mouth covered hers.

It was like coming home.

I've missed you so. It was a cry from her heart. In the few seconds of coherence before she was lost, Allison realized that she hadn't forgotten the passion that had overwhelmed her the night she spent with Jorge. She'd just refused to remember.

Now that feeling returned in an avalanche of emotion. She was swamped with a mix of love and desire so strong that she couldn't think, couldn't protest when he dragged her closer. He kissed her as if he was starved for the taste of her, the fingers of one hand threaded through her hair to shape her head and hold her still for the slow, erotic thrust of his tongue against hers.

Allison shuddered, her fingers closing into fists over the fine wool of his lapels.

The impatient blast of a truck horn shattered the spell that held them. Jorge lifted his head from hers, his eyes heavy-lidded, glittering behind the fringe of black lashes, and turned his head to look behind them.

He bit off a curse, his arms tightening in instinctive rejection of the need to let her go. Then he eased her off his lap and back to her seat.

"We're parked in a loading zone and there's a furniture truck behind us."

Allison could only nod at his explanation, disoriented from the sudden transition from passion to sanity.

"I'll walk you to the door."

Jorge thrust open the door and rounded the car to pull open the passenger door. Allison left the warm cave of the car and stepped out into the chilly, brisk air that was thankfully free of raindrops. She was grateful for the shelter of Jorge's body when he tucked her against his side, walked her to the building and into the relative warmth of the entryway.

"I won't come up," he said. "I'd be tempted to stay and you need to sleep."

His hand still rested on her waist as he turned her to face him, brushed his fingertips over her temple and tucked her hair behind her ear, then bent to press his mouth against hers for one fleeting moment.

"I'll pick you up tomorrow at lunch. We'll get the wedding license, then I'll feed you, okay?"

Allison murmured her assent. Jorge waited until she let herself into the building before he turned and left; she stood motionless, watching him through the glass in the old-fashioned door as he moved quickly down the steps, entered his car and drove off. It wasn't until the lumbering furniture truck pulled into the empty parking spot that she turned and climbed the stairs to the fourth floor.

Her apartment was blessedly warm. Allison hung up her coat and headed for the bedroom, shedding her suit and heels for the comfort of knit pajama pants and a long-sleeved top. Despite the tiredness that had dragged at her all afternoon, she was wide awake now. She turned down the bed, then padded into the kitchen to brew a mug of green tea. While she waited for the kettle to boil, she took a carton of yogurt from the refrigerator and ate it slowly, preoccupied with her thoughts.

If she'd entertained any thoughts that the sexual chemistry between them had faded in the weeks since the night she'd spent with Jorge, kissing him had proven her wrong. The connection between them was every bit as explosive as she'd remembered. Perhaps stronger, because now she knew where those heart-pounding kisses could lead.

She frowned, her hand pausing in midair with a spoonful of creamy strawberry yogurt.

Was it a good thing, or a bad thing, that they obviously shared a powerful chemistry? True, sex may be a bond that drew them closer together, but was that enough for a successful marriage?

Not likely, she acknowledged. They still moved in different worlds—and she wasn't the sort of woman to keep him enthralled with sex forever. Especially since she was going to grow bigger with the baby. On the other hand… She frowned, absentmindedly popping the spoon in her mouth and swallowing the yogurt without tasting it. She'd assumed that night with Jorge was the result of too much champagne and an uncharacteristic, reckless abandon on her part. Was it really, or had the passion and headlong sensuality she'd experienced been a product of meeting the right man? What if she really was capable of repeating the magic of that night? What if mind-blowing sex was the natural result of the potent chemistry that sparked between them? And what if it would always happen when she and Jorge were together?

Behind her, the kettle whistled, recalling her to the everyday normalcy of her small kitchenette, with its stack of law books waiting on the table.

She sighed and switched off the kettle. Moments later, carrying her mug of hot tea and a thick volume on contract law, she headed back to the bed-

room where she plumped the pillows against the
headboard and crawled into bed.

The following day she once again sat across the
table from Jorge in a restaurant, steaming plates on
the table in front of them.

"Should I have Laurie make arrangements with
a moving company to transfer your things to my
apartment this weekend?"

Allison froze. "No. Thank you."

He eyed her across the width of the small table.
"We haven't discussed where we'll live, but since
my place is bigger than yours, I assumed that you'd
move in with me. I have a two-bedroom apartment
on the Upper West Side. I'm using the second bedroom as an office at the moment, but we can clear
it out and turn it into a nursery for the baby."

The thought of moving in with him was daunting.
Not that Allison hadn't thought about it. She had.
But coming on the heels of obtaining the license
that made the approaching marriage official, the
idea was intimidating.

"I don't have anything packed," she began. His
eyes narrowed as she continued, "I haven't had
time, and to be honest, I don't know when I'll find
time in the next week or two."

"The next week or two?" he repeated slowly.
His jaw tightened. He gave up all pretense of eating
and leaned back in his chair, his gaze assessing.

"When, exactly, do you think you'll find time to pack?"

"I don't know. I haven't thought about it." She lifted her chin, returning his stare.

"Well, I suggest you think about it now." A hint of steel underlaid his deep tones.

Allison knew she had to address the issue of where they would live, and on some level she also knew she was being unreasonable, but she didn't like being pushed into a decision. No matter how politely it was done, she didn't like feeling cornered.

"I will." Her words were even, deliberate. He acknowledged them with a further narrowing of his eyes, and a muscle flexed in his jaw. He stared at her for a long, charged moment before he shifted and abruptly picked up his glass and drank.

"Are you sure you don't want your parents at the ceremony?" he asked, changing the subject so completely that Allison blinked in surprise.

"Yes, I'm very sure. Their schedules are always extremely busy. I'll call them after the ceremony, perhaps they'll meet us for dinner on their next trip to New York." She avoided his gaze by focusing intently on cutting a small, bite-size piece from an asparagus spear.

"I'll look forward to meeting them."

His words were expressionless. Allison glanced

up at him, but he was cutting his steak and she couldn't read his eyes.

It occurred to her that she had no idea if he was inviting family to the wedding.

"Will your parents be at the wedding?"

"Unfortunately, no. My mother's out of town and my father passed away some time ago."

"Oh. I'm sorry."

He shrugged. "It was a long time ago."

"Then you must have been very young when you lost him," she ventured, suddenly aware that she knew very little about his family. *How can I marry a man I know so little about?*

Panic fluttered in her midsection. She laid down her fork, picking up her glass to sip water and give her uneasy tummy time to settle.

"I was eight."

"Oh, Jorge." Shock and sympathy that he had lost a parent at such a tender age flooded her. "How did it happen?"

"He was killed in a convenience store robbery in Brooklyn."

"That's terrible." Allison shook her head, stunned at the words.

"Yes, it was," Jorge murmured, watching her face. "We stopped in for a gallon of milk and it cost him his life."

"We?" Allison was aghast. "Were you with him?"

"Yes."

Without thinking, she impulsively reached across the table, covering his hand with hers. "What an awful thing for a child to see."

He threaded his fingers through hers, his thumb drawing lazy circles on the sensitive skin of her palm.

"It was a long time ago, Allison."

"But it must have had a tremendous impact on you, not only to lose your father when you were so young, but to lose him in such a violent way."

"I suppose so." He glanced down at their entwined hands. "I swore that when I grew up, I'd do everything I could to keep that from happening to another family." He looked up, his gaze thoughtful as he searched her face. "I suppose that's why I became a district attorney—so I could put criminals in jail and keep as many of them as possible out of convenience stores."

A small smile curved his mouth. Allison's heart jolted, her breath caught.

"That's a very good reason to be an attorney," she said softly, her own lips curving irresistibly upward in response to his.

"I think you're right," he acknowledged. "And you?" he prompted. "Why do you want to become an attorney?"

"I want to make a difference in the world, to

protect innocent children and animals from the bad things in the world that can harm them.''

''Is that why you were at the save-the-whales fund-raiser?''

Allison laughed. ''No, I went to the fund-raiser because Zoe told me I'd been living like a nun and dragged me out of my apartment.''

''Remind me to tell Zoe thank you.''

''I will,'' she murmured, her pulse beating faster at the heat in his dark eyes.

Jorge lay awake late that night, thinking about the soft, melting look in Allison's amber eyes when he'd turned her hand over and kissed her palm.

Despite her quick retreat behind polite wariness when the waiter approached with the dessert menu, he was satisfied that he'd made a start at reaching beyond the emotional walls she hid behind. Combined with the kiss they'd shared in the car in front of her apartment the night before, her softening at the restaurant had him feeling far more confident that he would eventually knock down her walls completely.

The drapes were open, allowing light and shadow to dance across the ceiling. He frowned at the white plaster, following the flicker of light and dark without knowing he did so. His thoughts turned inward, remembering her laughter at lunch, her earnest answer when he'd asked her why she wanted to be an attorney. Those moments when she was relaxed and comfortable with him gave him hope, for he'd caught glimpses of the Allison he'd spent that unforgettable night with. That was the Allison he wanted to find again.

Chapter Five

The peal of the doorbell woke Allison on Saturday morning. She opened one eye, peered at the clock, groaned and closed her eyes again. The doorbell rang again and she pulled a pillow over her head.

Someone knocked on the door, then rang the bell, then knocked again.

"That has to be Zoe." Allison shoved the pillow and blankets aside and sat up, pushing her hair out of her eyes and yawning as she found her slippers and caught up her robe from the foot of the bed. She shrugged into the blue terry cloth robe, tying it around her as she crossed the living room, and paused with one hand on the doorknob, belatedly remembering to be cautious. "Who is it?"

"Zoe. Let me in."

Allison pulled open the door, and Zoe whisked past her.

"It's about time you woke up. Did you stay out late partying last night, I hope?"

Allison laughed as she pushed the door closed and walked past Zoe, heading for the kitchen. "No." She yawned and pulled open the cabinet to take out the coffee can.

"No?" Zoe set a jar of jam on the small table, then pulled out one of the dinette chairs and sat, propping her chin on her hand and eyeing Allison with interest. "Then what were you doing? Please tell me you were doing something fun—don't tell me you stayed up late studying again."

"Well, I was studying…"

Zoe groaned and rolled her eyes.

"But I haven't been studying the entire time you've been gone. Is that from your mom?" Allison pointed at the jar on the table.

"Yes. Raspberry jam. And don't try to distract me. Tell me what you've been doing while I've been gone."

"It's a long story." Allison poured water into the coffeemaker and measured decaf blend into the filter.

"I have all day," Zoe said promptly.

Allison switched the brew button on and faced Zoe, leaning back against the counter. "Do you remember Jorge, the man I left the save-the-whales fund-raiser with?''

''You mean the gorgeous, tall, dark and sexy guy?'' Zoe grinned impishly. ''Oh, yeah, I remember him. He was pretty unforgettable. What about him?''

''He came by the office to see me. We've had lunch a couple of times.''

''Excellent!'' Delighted, Zoe leaned forward. ''And?'' she prompted, ''Are you going to see him again?''

''Yes. We're getting married next week. I want you to be my maid of honor.''

Zoe's eyes widened and she blinked slowly. ''Say that again? Because I must have misunderstood what you just said. I thought you said you're getting married next week.''

''I did. I am.''

The shock and disbelief on Zoe's face were easily readable. Allison knew that evasive answers wouldn't work with Zoe; her friend would never settle for less than the truth. Zoe's mouth opened and Allison held up a hand.

''Coffee first, Zoe, then I'll explain everything.''

Zoe jumped up and opened the cupboard next to Allison, took out two mugs and, with complete disregard for the coffeemaker, expertly yanked out the pot and substituted one of the mugs beneath the slow stream of black brew. She filled the remaining mug with steaming hot coffee and handed it to Allison.

"Sit."

Allison took a chair at the table while Zoe repeated the fast switch of coffeepot for mug, then plopped into the chair opposite.

"Okay, you have coffee. Tell me everything."

Allison laughed. "I need to actually swallow the coffee and wake up first."

Zoe waved a hand dismissingly. "This is decaf. It won't do a thing to jump-start your brain. So talk."

"I spent the night with Jorge after the fundraiser."

Zoe's eyes rounded with surprise. "You're kidding!"

"No, I'm not kidding." Allison tucked her sleep-ruffled hair behind her ears and picked up her mug, sipping slowly. Even though she knew that the coffee held no caffeine, the morning ritual eased her a few inches toward being completely awake. "I'm pregnant."

"Geez." Zoe gasped, her eyes widening once again.

"Jorge and I decided to marry—for the sake of the baby."

"You're kidding?" Zoe shook her head in amazement. "The men I know would all head for the nearest exit if I told them I was pregnant."

"I thought that's exactly what Jorge would do. In fact, I hadn't decided if I was ever going to tell him about the baby, but I accidentally let it slip."

"You accidentally told him you were pregnant?" Zoe tucked one leg beneath her on the chair seat and settled comfortably. "Start at the beginning and tell me everything. Don't leave anything out."

"...and the wedding is set for next week," Allison finished, several moments later. "Jorge knows a judge who will perform the ceremony in his chambers."

"Wow. I leave town for a week and look what happens." Zoe stared at her, amazement written across her features. "Before I left, it was almost impossible to talk you into leaving this apartment to go grocery shopping, and when I return, you're about to marry one of the most powerful attorneys in New York City." She frowned. "Which reminds me, why didn't you tell me the gorgeous guy you were with at the fund-raiser was Jorge Perez?"

"Because I didn't connect the name until later." Though they'd shared last names, Allison hadn't realized until much too late that her Jorge was the same Jorge Perez featured in media coverage of high-profile criminal cases. She should have connected his name with the district attorney's office immediately, but she'd been too distracted by the man himself.

"How could you possibly not have known?"

Zoe's expressive eyebrows winged upward in surprise. "You're in law school, don't you follow the current big cases?"

"Not nearly as much as I should." Allison waved her hand at the piles of law books that covered half the table. "I'm so buried with studying, on top of the hours I spend at Manhattan Multiples, that I sometimes don't have time to do more than read headlines of the daily newspaper or catch more than a few minutes of the nightly news on television."

She stood and retrieved the coffeepot, returning to the table to refill both mugs. Zoe's eyes narrowed speculatively, and Allison paused, instinctively covering her tummy with one hand.

"What?"

"Nothing. I'm just looking to see if you're showing yet. But I don't see a difference. Do you?"

"Not yet." She turned away to replace the pot of coffee, then slipped back into her chair. "Except that I had to buy new bras. All of mine were suddenly too small."

"Wow," Zoe murmured, sipping her coffee. "You're going to have big changes in your life, Allison. A baby on the way, a new husband. Probably a new home, since this apartment is too small for three people. Where are you going to live?"

"Jorge has a two-bedroom apartment. I think he expects us to live there."

"You think? Don't you know?"

"We haven't really had a chance to decide."

Zoe pursed her lips and eyed her. "Well you better decide fast, Allison. When you come home from the honeymoon, where are the two of you sleeping?"

Trust Zoe to cut to the heart of the matter. Allison thrust her fingers through her hair and twisted a strand around her forefinger, chewing her lip.

"You wouldn't rather stay here, would you?" Zoe's gaze made a swift survey of the tiny kitchen and the small living room beyond.

Allison's glance followed Zoe's and she sighed. "No. I like my apartment but it's barely big enough for one, let alone two more." She frowned, staring unseeingly at her cup.

"Then what's the problem? If Jorge has a bigger apartment, it seems obvious that you should move in with him."

"Yes, I suppose it does." Allison's insides clenched at the thought of moving in with Jorge. It was the logical choice, yet she was reluctant to give up her independence.

Zoe reached across the table, her hand closing with warm comfort over Allison's. "Hey, you told me that Jorge is a nice guy. He wants to do the right thing for you and the baby. You're going to have to trust him."

A sudden rush of emotion brought tears to Allison's eyes. "I know. It's just…it's hard, you know?"

"I know." Zoe knew only too well how guarded Allison was, how careful she was to protect her heart. She patted Allison's hand. "But you have to, if this marriage is going to have a chance." She waited until Allison nodded. "And if gorgeous Jorge disappoints us, I'll call the twins."

Allison laughed, a watery sound halfway between a chuckle and a sob. The twins were two men that frequented the coffee bar where Zoe worked. Tall, blond, muscled hulks who worked as computer programmers during the day and moonlighted as wrestlers at night, they adored Zoe and extended their protection to her friends.

Zoe left to get ready for work after sharing breakfast with Allison and deciding what she would wear to the wedding as maid of honor. Allison showered, dressed and was deeply immersed in studying when the doorbell rang once again.

Thinking that Zoe must have forgotten something, Allison pulled open her door. Jorge stood in the hallway. The beautiful suits she'd always seen him in before were absent, replaced by worn Levi's, black boots, and a black T-shirt under a deep brown leather bomber jacket. His black hair was ruffled and dark beard stubble shadowed his jaw. He looked faintly disreputable, rough and altogether too sexy for Allison's peace of mind.

"Hi."

"Hi." She stared at him, bemused. "Did we have a date?"

"No." He looked past her and into her apartment, then glanced down the hall behind him. "Can I come in?"

"Oh, yes. Of course." Flustered, she stepped back, and he moved past her and into the living room. When she closed the door and turned to him, he was so close to her that the curve of her breasts brushed his jacket. He slipped an arm around her waist, nudged her back against the door and covered her mouth with his.

Allison didn't have time to think, only to feel. She went from calm to passionate in seconds, seduced by the urgency of his mouth and the hard length of his body pressing hers against the door at her back.

Long before she was ready, he lifted his head and looked down at her. One hard thigh was wedged between hers, and her arms circled his neck, her fingers in his hair, her body pressed tightly against his.

Jorge looked into Allison's flushed face, her eyes dazed, her mouth faintly swollen from the pressure of his, and felt a surge of satisfaction.

"What are you doing this afternoon?" He traced the curve of her cheekbone with soft, butterfly kisses, and she closed her eyes, catching her breath, until he stopped just below her ear.

"Studying. Why?"

"Play hooky for a while. I want to show you something."

Her eyes lost some of their passion-glazed look, but she didn't push him away. "What is it?"

"A surprise. Can't tell you. You have to see it." He easily read the indecision on her expressive features. "Come on," he murmured. "I'll help you study after I bring you home."

He bent, nuzzling the soft skin of her throat just below her ear. She sighed and tipped her head back against the door, allowing him access.

"All right." Her voice was faint. "But I can't be gone for long, I really have to study today."

He lifted his head and smiled at her. Just as he'd hoped, she was distracted by the sensual heat that blazed between them, so caught up in passion that she'd forgotten to be wary. There wasn't a shred of caution or fear in her amber eyes, and her body lay trustingly against his, her arms holding him close.

"It's a deal." He pressed one last, lingering kiss against her mouth and reluctantly eased away from her. "Grab your coat, it's cold outside."

Moments later they were in a taxi, weaving through Saturday afternoon traffic.

"Now will you tell me where we're going?"

"To my place." He grinned and smoothed his

forefinger over the two tiny frown lines that appeared between her brows. "But I can't tell you what the surprise is, you'll have to wait until we get there."

The look she gave him was suspicious, the faint wariness he always sensed in her unless she was diverted by passion visible in her eyes.

"Trust me. You'll like it."

She clearly reserved judgment, but they passed the taxi ride in general conversation about their week, the traffic, the weather and a variety of other safe topics. Jorge could see Allison tense when they left the taxi and entered his building. She barely spoke as they entered the elevator, her uneasiness palpable as the lift carried them upward to the nineteenth floor.

"After you."

She walked ahead of him out of the elevator, and he touched her arm to direct her to the left. "It's this way."

They halted at the end of the hallway and Jorge slipped a key into the lock, pushed the door open and stood back to let her enter.

"It's not very homey," he commented, his gaze following hers as she crossed the small entryway to look into the living area. He'd never given much thought to his apartment; it was just a place to sleep, eat, and work. He had a cleaning service that came in every week so it was scrubbed and neat, but as he walked behind Allison, he looked at it through her eyes and realized it was sterile. The cherry wood armoire that held the television, VCR/ DVD player and state-of-the-art stereo had video tapes of court cases stacked six deep on top. The leather sofa and matching ottoman next to the club chair had case files piled neatly on their smooth, chocolate brown surfaces.

There were no prints or photos on the stark-white walls. The best feature in the room was the large window that looked out on the landscape of the Upper West Side.

Allison hadn't said a word. She just stood in the center of the rug, her gaze sliding slowly over the room and its furnishings. Jorge wondered what she was thinking, but he couldn't read her expression. She was absorbed in the apartment, unaware that he stared at the clean lines of her profile, the smooth line of her brow and the sweep of richly colored hair framing her face, the line of her small nose, the plush curve of lips and the small chin beneath, the vulnerable inward curve of throat and delicate collarbone. His heart lurched, settled back into a faster rhythm. He wanted to pick her up and carry her into the bedroom, the need to cherish her mixed with pounding lust. He wanted her in his bed again, naked, willing, needing him as badly as he needed her. He had to know that she desired him with the same fierce compulsion that made him crave her.

She turned, her gaze pausing to meet his before moving on to slip over the walls of the entry behind him.

"You can change anything you want," he said, shrugging in apology. "I always planned to buy more furniture and hang a few pictures, but I never got around to it."

"It has much more room than my apartment," she said diplomatically.

"Well, that's something, I guess." He gave her a wry smile, and she smiled back tentatively. Encouraged, he closed the space between them and caught her hand in his to tug her down the short hall. "The rest of the rooms are decent sizes. This is the main bedroom." He waved a hand at the first door that stood open, allowing a glimpse of plush, cream-colored carpet, king-size bed, one nightstand and a dresser. "There's a bathroom off the bedroom, and another one here." He paused for a moment to let her peer into a large, gleaming bathroom with white and dark-blue tiles. "And this is the room that I thought we could make into a nursery."

He pushed open the door and stepped inside, drawing Allison with him. He knew the instant she saw the rocking chair and the stuffed Gund teddy bear that nearly filled the glossy oak seat, for her eyes widened and she caught her breath. Her hand tightened around his, and the smile she turned on him was heartfelt, her eyes misty, the wariness that normally lurked there erased by her delighted surprise.

"Oh, Jorge."

"Do you like it?"

"I love it." She moved quickly across the room, stroking a hand down the curved arm of the high-backed rocker. "Where did you find it?"

"At an antique shop in the Village."

"And the teddy bear?" She picked the big bear out of the chair and cuddled him, the caramel-colored, stuffed plush legs dangling to her knees.

"I found him in a toy store downtown." He frowned, measuring the size of the big bear against Allison's slim form. "He's kind of big. Think the baby will like him? Maybe I should have gotten a smaller one."

Allison laughed and rubbed her cheek against the bear's fuzzy head. "I think the baby will love him, but it might be a while before she can pick him up."

"Yeah." He thrust his hand through his hair and then propped his hands on his hips, his gaze flicking assessingly over the desk, chair and bookcase that were the room's only other furniture. "I'll move this stuff out of here and you can decorate it however you want. I looked at cribs and other baby furniture but had no idea what you wanted, so I didn't buy anything. We can go shopping whenever you have a Saturday free from studying."

"Okay." Allison dropped into the chair, the teddy bear on her lap, and rocked gently, a small smile curving her lips, one hand tracing the gleaming grain of the wood on the chair arm.

Jorge looked at her, his heart tightening. "You really do like it, don't you?"

"Yes." Her smile warmed. "I like it a lot. What made you go shopping for a rocking chair?"

"I wasn't exactly shopping for a chair. I walked past the store, and the chair was in the window." He shrugged dismissively, unwilling to tell her that he'd had an instant mental image of her sitting in the chair, their baby at her breast. He'd walked straight into the shop and paid an exorbitant amount for the chair without hesitation.

"And the teddy bear?" Her amber eyes smiled at him, gently teasing.

He grinned. "I admit I went looking for the bear. Not for such a big bear, but this guy grabbed my attention the minute I walked through the door of F.A.O. Schwarz."

"I can see why," she said dryly. "I'm guessing that as big as he is, you could hardly see the normal-size bears."

"He did sort of dominate the stuffed animal section." Jorge enjoyed the accord that lay between them, loath to disrupt the quiet pleasure in Allison's expression. But they had little time before the wedding and far too many issues to resolve. "So, do you think you'll like living here?'' His voice was serious, stripped of the earlier teasing note as he tried to read the shift of emotions across her features. She looked away, her gaze moving around the room, touching on the furniture, the bare walls, the view out the window.

''I know I'll have to give up my apartment when we're married, Jorge. After all, the reason we're marrying is so that we can share our child, and I don't want you to miss the months before she's born,'' she said finally. ''But I'm neither ready nor willing to move in here with you before the ceremony.'' She looked back at him, her amber eyes determined, a faint hint of appeal in her voice. ''My life is in complete chaos right now and I haven't begun to come to terms with all the changes.''

Jorge looked at her, silently weighing her words. The sunlight poured through the window beside her, highlighting the fragility of bones and the vulnerability of her expression.

Was he pushing her too hard, too fast? Maybe he should back off, give her time to come to terms with their marriage and living together. He was reluctant to give her physical space because that was the one area in which he was reassured that she wanted him as much as he wanted her. Still, he thought, there were only five more days until the ceremony. And given the speed with which he'd made plans, surely five days wasn't too much to ask.

"All right." He was rewarded with a swift smile of relief from Allison. "I'll make arrangements to have the movers empty your apartment and transfer your belongings while we're gone. That way you won't have to worry about packing and unpacking because by the time we get home, everything will be set up here."

"Get home? From where?"

Jorge nearly groaned aloud. "Damn. I'm sorry. I should have told you—Judge Maddock has a free hour on Thursday so the wedding is set for 1:00 p.m., and a friend has loaned me his cabin upstate for the weekend, or longer, if you can get away from work and classes."

"Thursday?" Panic flooded Allison. Thursday was only five days away. Five short days and she'd be married. You knew the ceremony would be next week, she reminded herself.

"Is Thursday okay with you?" Jorge asked. "You don't have anything scheduled that day that you can't postpone, do you?"

"No. No, Thursday is fine." The panic subsided, helped by several purposely deep breaths. Then the rest of his comment registered and panic surged again. "We're going away after the wedding?"

"Yes. My boss has a cabin upstate. It's on the edge of a small town with several good restaurants, and the cabin itself is in the woods, with a stream running outside the back door. Very quiet and relaxing.''

"I hadn't realized we were going away after the wedding," she said faintly.

"I thought we could use a break after the last few weeks. Can you get away for a week?"

Allison shook her head. "I have a class on Tuesday night that I can't possibly miss."

"What about Thursday night? Friday?"

"My classes are on Monday and Tuesday nights, so the rest of the week is free."

"Great, then we can leave after the ceremony on Thursday and return Monday morning."

Allison wanted to refuse, but something in his eyes made her pause. "All right." The swift flare of satisfaction in his dark gaze stirred an urge to run, far and fast. She rose from the chair and carefully returned the giant teddy bear to his former seat before she moved toward the door and the hallway beyond. "If a moving company is going to pack and move me next week, I have a lot of things to take care of at my apartment. I should go home and get started."

He followed her down the hall and out the door, her senses prickling with anticipation. But he didn't take her arm, didn't take the opportunity to kiss her again while they were alone in his apartment. He fairly radiated a leashed sensual energy that had her on edge as he stalked behind her and into the elevator, but he kept a careful twelve inches between their bodies.

By the time they reached her apartment, Allison was strung so taut with expectation that she was nearly quivering. Her hands trembled and she fumbled with the key, frustrated when she missed the lock.

"Here, let me."

Jorge reached around her and took the key from her unresisting hand, slipping it into the lock to open the door. She stepped over the threshold and turned, holding the edge of the door. His gaze was brooding, his hands tucked into his jeans pockets, the bomber jacket unbuttoned and open over his chest.

"Do you want me to come in and help you study?"

She shook her head. "Thanks, Jorge, but I think I'll take a short nap and then make a list for Zoe so she can organize the movers next weekend."

"All right." His gaze searched her face, lingering on her mouth. "I'll call you later."

"Sure."

"Allison…"

"Yes?"

"Nothing. I'll call."

He turned and strode down the hall. Seconds later Allison heard his boots thudding against the stair treads as he descended. Bewildered, she closed the door, slipped out of her coat and put it away.

He didn't kiss me goodbye.

Though she dreaded his kisses—because she lost control—as much as she craved them for their hot addictive pleasure, she felt oddly bereft that he'd left without kissing her. It occurred to her to wonder if he was already tired of her.

"Stop it," she muttered aloud, thrusting her fingers through her hair, exasperated. "This isn't a love match. Get over it."

Determinedly she marched into the kitchen to find a pen and pad of paper for list making. But a tiny part of her wept for the likelihood that her soon-to-be husband didn't love her, and could already be tiring of her uncertainty and wildly vacillating emotions.

The days flew by, so packed with her busy schedule at work, studying, organizing her apartment into what could be moved to Jorge's apartment and what should go into storage, that Allison barely had a moment to fret over whether Jorge would ever grow to care for her. Fortunately, it also left little time for her to analyze her own feelings toward Jorge.

Thursday morning dawned bright, cold and clear. Allison woke early and, unable to go back to sleep, rose to pack her bag for the weekend. Zoe knocked on her door at ten-thirty sharp.

"Hi-ya." She breezed past Allison into the apartment and turned to inspect her. "You aren't dressed."

Allison glanced down at her jeans and T-shirt, her feet comfortable in white socks. "I know. I'm finishing packing a box of kitchen things." She walked into the kitchen. "My refrigerator is almost empty, but will you take the orange juice and milk?"

Zoe followed her, her gaze skimming the packed cardboard boxes stacked neatly in the tiny kitchen. "You've been busy," she commented.

"I woke up at five this morning and couldn't go back to sleep," Allison confessed. She scanned the kitchen and pulled open cupboard doors and drawers to verify that they were empty, then glanced at the clock. "I think it's time to get dressed."

"Yes." Zoe arched a brow and grinned at her. "From the state of your kitchen, I'd say you've put it off as long as you can."

Allison's nerves eased and she laughed ruefully. "At least packing kept me busy and kept my mind off the wedding."

"Are you horribly nervous?" Zoe followed her into the bedroom and perched on the bed to watch Allison pull open a dresser drawer and remove a cream-colored satin bra and panties edged with deep bands of delicate lace. "Because you can still change your mind."

Allison pushed the drawer closed. "I know." She met Zoe's worried gaze with relative calm. "I won't deny that knowing I'm marrying today terrifies me, but I'm convinced that this is the best thing for my baby. And Jorge seems as committed as I am to making a good life for our child." She drew a deep breath and managed a smile. "So, I'm getting married."

"All-righty, then." Zoe waved her toward the bathroom. "Jump in the shower. We've barely got enough time to do your hair, make sure your makeup is perfect, and get you dressed. Scoot. Hurry."

Allison hurried. Having Zoe's bubbly personality to occupy her mind was a godsend. The butterflies in her stomach didn't return to take up residence until the car Jorge had sent to pick up Zoe and her dropped them at the courthouse.

She managed to ignore those butterflies until she and Zoe were shown into the anteroom of the Judge's chambers. Both women slipped out of their coats and used the mirror above a bookcase to check their hair and makeup.

"Are you sure I look okay?" Allison smoothed her palm down the lightweight wool cream skirt. The suit had a waist-length jacket, the whole image tasteful and chic. The silk sweater beneath the jacket hugged her curves, the square neckline revealing the beginning swell of breasts and the valley between. With the jacket buttoned, the matching sweater was unremarkable, but without the jacket, it was blatantly sexy and very different from her usual tailored businesswear. A matching handbag and pumps had been delivered with the suit. Allison wasn't entirely comfortable with knowing that Jorge had bought her clothing, especially since the ensemble reminded her of the very glamorous black evening gown she'd worn the first time they met. Did he still see her this way? Sophisticated and sexy? Even though she was pregnant?

"You look absolutely fabulous," Zoe said promptly. "I think these are for you."

Allison turned from the mirror to find Zoe holding out a bouquet of dark-red and white roses, creamy lilies and lacy greenery, tied with a deep-red satin ribbon.

"Oh, they're lovely." Tears welled up as Allison took the bouquet and brushed her lips against the cool petals, breathing in their sweet fragrance. "Where did you get them?"

"On the table." Zoe pointed to a small table just inside the door leading to the judge's chambers. "There's one for me, too. It seems your Jorge thought of everything."

"He has, hasn't he?" Allison felt a small stab of guilt that she'd allowed him to arrange the entire wedding.

A soft rap sounded on the door panels, and a

second later a young woman eased open the door to peer in.

"Miss Baker?" she queried, her gaze admiring as she smiled at the two women. "Judge Maddock is ready for you whenever you're ready to begin."

Allison drew a deep breath, and her gaze met Zoe's before she nodded. "Is Jorge here?"

"Yes, he's with the judge."

Allison was immensely grateful for Zoe's supportive presence at her elbow and slightly behind her as she entered the judge's chambers.

Jorge was across the room, talking to the judge and another man, his back to her.

"Ah, here's the bride." The white-haired man in black robes looked over Jorge's shoulder and smiled warmly.

Jorge immediately turned and went perfectly still. Allison's steps faltered as his gaze ran swiftly over her, his eyes dark and hot as they met hers once more. Then he strode across the room and took her hand, tucking her arm through his and covering her fingers with his palm, tight against the fine wool of his suit sleeve.

"Are you okay?" he bent his head to murmur, his lips brushing her ear.

She shivered in reaction, heat flashing swiftly through her veins.

"Yes," she managed. "I'm fine."

"Ready to do this?"

She looked up at him, her gaze searching his. The hot intensity was gone from his eyes, replaced by reassurance.

"Yes." She drew a deep breath. "I'm ready."

"Good." He glanced up and smiled at Zoe. "You must be Zoe. It's a pleasure to meet you."

Zoe took his outstretched hand, her narrowed gaze searching his face as they shook hands. Whatever she found there evidently satisfied her, for she nodded, her features softening as she smiled. "It's a pleasure to meet you, as well."

"Let me introduce you both to my friends." Keeping Allison's arm through his, he took Zoe's elbow with his free hand and drew the two across the room. "Allison, Zoe, I'd like you both to meet Judge Maddock, who'll be performing the ceremony."

Allison and Zoe both exchanged murmured greetings with the Judge.

"And this is Ross Daly. He's acting as my best man. Ross, this is Allison and her friend Zoe Armbruster."

"It's a pleasure to meet you, Zoe, and especially you, Allison. My wife is out of town and couldn't be here today but she asked me to convey her apologies as well as her congratulations. She's looking forward to having you and Jorge over for dinner the moment you have a free evening."

Allison had seen television interviews and newspaper photos of the city's district attorney, but he was much taller in person, well over six feet, and radiated energy. He and Jorge shared that sense of leashed power and keen intelligence. He also had the ability to make her feel safe, a quality he shared with Jorge. She didn't stop to wonder why two such compelling men didn't seem threatening. Instead, she felt a rush of gratitude for his friendly support.

"How lovely of her to invite us. Please tell her that I hope we can join you soon."

The sweet, warm smile she gave Ross rocked Jorge. This was the Allison he'd only caught brief glimpses of since the night they spent together. But those flashes were enough to convince him that the warm, passionate women he'd met at the fundraiser was hiding beneath the cautious exterior she showed to the world. He was determined to make her smile like this all the time.

"Well then, shall we get started?" Judge Maddock took a slim, leather-bound book from his assistant. "If you'll stand here, Jorge, with Allison beside you. Yes, that's good. And you on the groom's right, Ross, while you stand on the far side of the bride, Ms. Armbruster." The four shifted positions, lining up in front of him and he nodded. "Excellent. Let us begin."

Allison fought to keep the trembling that shook her on the inside from showing on the outside. Last-minute nerves threatened her equilibrium. Was she doing the right thing? Should she take more time to decide if she really wanted to do this?

Jorge's fingers threaded through hers, warm and strong, immeasurably comforting, and her nerves steadied, the butterflies in her stomach ceasing their fluttering.

The judge's words were a blur, until Zoe reached out and took the bride's bouquet from her hand and Jorge turned to face her, taking both her hands in his.

"Repeat after me," the judge said. "I, Jorge Alejandro Perez…"

Jorge's gaze remained on her while he repeated the solemn vows. Then Ross handed him a ring and he slipped it on her hand. The platinum wedding band held six large diamonds and was followed by an exquisitely cut marquis diamond engagement ring. The center stone was banded on each side by three diamonds the same size as those on the wedding band. Allison's soft gasp was barely audible, but Jorge heard it. He lifted her hand to his lips and kissed the rings against her hand, then turned her hand over to press a kiss to her palm.

Tears burned, and it was all Allison could do not to cry. Her gaze searched his, bewildered. This was a set of wedding rings that should be given by a man to a cherished bride, not to a woman whom his own sense of honor and responsibility forced him to marry.

She would have protested, but it was too late. The judge was quoting her vows, and she repeated them, overwhelmed by the solemnity of the occasion.

"I'm sorry, I don't have a ring for you," she murmured, but Zoe interrupted before Jorge could respond, reaching around her to tuck a heavy platinum men's wedding band into her hand. Numbly Allison took it, slipping it over the knuckle of his third finger, left hand. She looked up, and Jorge's fingers tightened over hers as he drew her closer. She caught only a glimpse of fierce black eyes before he wrapped his arms around her and his mouth closed over hers.

The kiss was gentle, his mouth cherishing hers for long moments, and the tears that had trembled on her eyelashes spilled over to trail down her cheeks. When he lifted his head at last, he smoothed the dampness with his thumb and smiled tenderly.

"Hey, no tears. You're not supposed to be crying."

"I know." She stepped back, brushing at the tears. "I seem to be crying at every little thing lately. I'm happy, really I am."

Chapter Six

Allison fell asleep before the Jag drove out of New York City. The nearly sleepless night, added to the weariness induced by the baby's impact on her body, kept her asleep until the car stopped, the engine was switched off and Jorge shook her gently awake.

"Allison. Allison?"

"Mmm." Disoriented, she opened sleepy eyes to find him outside the car, the passenger door open as he leaned across her to unlatch her seat belt. "Where are we?"

"At the cabin." Jorge deftly eased the seat belt away and slipped his arms beneath her to pick her up, neatly swinging her clear of the car and nudging the door closed with his hip.

"I slept the entire trip?" Allison was dismayed.

"Yes. You must have been exhausted. Have you been sleeping at night?"

"Not last night," she confessed, lifting her head from his shoulder to look about them. Red and gold leaves littered the ground and crunched beneath his shoes as he carried her along the path between car and porch. He climbed the shallow, wide steps to the front door and, without releasing her, slipped the key into the lock and pushed the door inward.

He carried her inside and kicked the door shut.

"Oh, this is lovely." Allison's gaze moved over the room. A river-rock fireplace took up one wall, a comfortable upholstered blue sofa, love seat and matching armchair ranged in front of the hearth. On each side of the fireplace, long windows overlooked the woods behind the house. Blue drapes framed the glass panes, echoing the deep blue of sofa and pillows. A small grand piano took up one corner, its gleaming black surface holding a collection of photos in silver frames that were all sizes. More family photos hung on the wall behind the piano, side by side with a beautiful old oil painting of woods in winter. "When you told me that we were going to a cabin in the woods, I thought you meant a rustic little getaway. This is a beautiful home."

Jorge grinned. "Ross and Sarah started out with

drawings for a little cabin in the woods, but they fell in love with the land and decided to build a bigger, more permanent home here. They spend several months here every year. The kids are crazy about it. They'd rather come here than go to Disneyland."

"I don't blame them."

Jorge walked across the living room and let Allison peek into the kitchen. "I called the local family that takes care of the cabin for Ross, and they promised to stock the refrigerator and fill the wood box."

He turned and retraced his steps, crossing the living room to stride down the hallway past two doors before he stopped at the end of the hall.

"This is the master bedroom. There's a bathroom through there." He indicated a door at the far side of the room, banked on each side by closet doors, before crossing the wood floors to the bed. He paused and looked down at her, his gaze searching her features, noting the faint circles that underlined her eyes despite her nap in the car. "Why don't you rest while I unload the car."

"But I slept through the entire drive here," Allison protested. "And it was terribly rude of me. I'm sorry, I just can't seem to stay awake for long."

"Don't worry about it. I know the last week has been busy for you, add that to the toll the baby is taking on your energy and you've got good reason to feel tired.''

She eyed him solemnly. ''You're being very nice to me.''

He quirked an eyebrow, a slow smile lifting the corners of his mouth. ''I've got an ulterior motive.''

''Really?'' Allison's heart raced. ''And what is that?''

''I'm a lousy cook, and I'm hoping that if you get lots of rest, you'll have the energy to help me make dinner.''

Allison laughed. His answer was so far removed from the one she'd been expecting that it caught her completely off guard.

''I think I can manage that.''

''Good.'' He swung her to her feet next to the bed and leaned over to tug the pillow free and sweep back the heavy silk spread, blanket and sheet. He finished and looked at her, his gaze sweeping her from head to toe. ''Want some help getting out of that suit?''

''No. Thank you.'' She felt heat move up her throat and cheeks as his gaze returned to hers, his dark eyes heavy-lidded and heated. ''I think I can manage.''

''I'm sure you can. That's not what I asked.'' His gaze was wry. ''But we'll pick this up later.'' He bent and pressed a quick hard kiss to her mouth. ''Sleep well, angel.''

Before Allison could respond, he was gone, the door closing quietly behind him. Allison didn't know if she was glad that he didn't press her, or not. She craved physical contact with him, her body and heart responding every time he touched her. The feeling constantly surprised her, for she'd avoided men completely since that night when she was seventeen and had attended an award after-party with her parents. Dressed in a designer gown that made her look much older than her years, she was starry-eyed and elated when a rising young actor that she'd dreamed about for months went out of his way to charm her. With too much alcohol in his system, he'd lured her into a private room, seduced and then forced her when she'd tried to stop him. Devastated, she was further traumatized when she later learned that he'd only been attentive to her because he wanted a part in her father's next production.

She'd never told her parents about that night; in fact, she'd never confided her darkest secret to anyone. Instead she avoided men and dressed in conservative clothes that played down her feminine features.

Until the night she went to the fund-raiser and met Jorge.

Had he been attracted to her because of the dress, glamorous hair and makeup? Or would he have wanted her if he'd first seen her in her conservative business suits?

And was it only that she'd been feeling uncharacteristically reckless that night that she'd shed her fear of men and welcomed his touch? He'd slipped past her defenses without her once trying to stop him, she thought, and hadn't ever triggered the panic that had made her avoid male contact.

Too tired to work it out, she stripped off the suit jacket and skirt and hung them up in the large closet, slipped the silk sweater onto a padded hanger and crawled into bed. She was asleep almost instantly.

She awoke several hours later. The afternoon was gone and the world outside the bedroom window was dark. Refreshed, Allison slipped from the bed and went into the bathroom. Her hair was tangled and she grimaced at the smudged makeup beneath her eyes and the lack of color on her lips and cheeks. She returned to the bedroom and took fresh underwear, a soft, blue cashmere sweater and jeans from the suitcase at the foot of the bed, carrying them with her back into the bathroom where she turned on the shower.

She paused while stripping off her lace panties, arrested by the sight of diamonds glittering on her left hand. She kicked off her underwear and turned her hand in the light from the overhead fixture, admiring the gleam of diamonds and platinum.

She was still bemused and amazed that Jorge had bought her such beautiful, obviously expensive rings. She didn't think she'd ever seen an engagement ring and wedding band so appealing. Several moments went by before she shook herself and climbed into the shower.

A half hour later she was feeling much better. Hair blown dry, makeup reapplied, dressed in clean, casual clothing, she left the bedroom and padded down the hall to the lamplit living room. A quick, sweeping glance told her that Jorge wasn't there. But soft music and the sound of someone whistling came from the kitchen, and she crossed the living room to the doorway.

Jorge stood in front of the stove, his back to her. Delta blues wailed softly from the CD player in a corner shelf unit, and he whistled in time with the saxophone. He wore blue jeans, faded and well-worn at stress points, with a white T-shirt tucked into the waistband. White socks covered his feet and his black hair gleamed, damp from a shower.

He turned away from the stove, opening a drawer to take out a large spoon, and saw her. A slow smile curved his mouth, and Allison's toes curled against the wood floor, her nerves tightening with anticipation.

"Hi." His voice was a shade deeper than usual, huskier.

"Hi." She couldn't look away from the growing

heat in his eyes. Her heart picked up a beat, thudding harder, faster.

"I wondered if you were going to sleep the night through."

"What time is it?" She glanced around the kitchen, locating a digital readout on the microwave above the stove. The lit dials read ten minutes after eight. "It's after eight o'clock? That can't be right."

"Oh, but it is. You must have been worn-out. Did you sleep at all last night?"

"Not very much. I didn't go to bed until after eleven, and then tossed and turned until I finally gave up trying to sleep around 5:00 a.m."

"Did knowing we were getting married today keep you awake? Were you having second thoughts?"

She could have lied to him and said no. But something about the direct question and his steady gaze made her respond in kind. "Yes." A small frown creased his brow and his jaw tightened. "And no," she hastened to add. "It wasn't just getting married. It was everything, the baby, becoming a mother, getting married." She broke off, gesturing helplessly. "I like to plan my life, and this has all happened so fast. I found out that I was pregnant and we decided to marry so quickly that I haven't really had time to absorb all the changes that are sure to follow. I'm not sure I'm ready for all this.''

He didn't say anything, but his eyes narrowed in consideration. Silence stretched between them and Allison rushed in to fill it.

''I don't mean to sound negative or ungrateful. You've been terrific about this whole thing—wanting to be a father to our baby, making all the arrangements for the wedding, giving me beautiful rings. It's just that I feel as if I've been swept up in a tornado and then set down again, with my life entirely changed. I'm sure I'll adjust, but it will take a little time.'' She pushed her fingers through her hair in agitation. ''You seem so calm. Don't you feel any of this?''

''Sure.'' His voice was level, his features unreadable to Allison. ''But I'm not the one who's pregnant. The books I've read all warn that a woman's body goes through major changes when she's pregnant and that those changes can cause emotional swings that seem manic. Do you think there's a possibility that all of this will seem less overwhelming when your body adjusts to being pregnant?''

''I don't know. I hope so.'' She stared at him, arrested. ''The books you've read? You've read books on pregnancy?''

He shrugged, muscles flexing beneath the T-shirt, and streaks of color highlighting his cheekbones. ''I thought I should read a few so I'd have a basic idea of what to expect."

"Oh." Allison stared at him, a smile beginning. "That is so sweet, Jorge."

"It's not sweet," he growled. "I told you, I'm not sweet."

"Hmm." She smiled more widely, delighted by his embarrassment. "If you say so."

The oven timer went off with a buzz and he turned to pull open the door and peer inside.

"I think this is hot." He put aside the spoon, picked up two hot pads and bent to take a casserole out of the oven.

"What is it?" Allison crossed the tiled floor and peered around his shoulder at the bowl.

Jorge lifted the lid, and a fragrant cloud of steam rose from the hot bowl. "The note said it was French something or other, but it looks like plain, old beef stew to me."

"It smells heavenly."

"Are you hungry?" Jorge looked down at her, but before she could respond, her stomach growled. She felt her face flush, and he laughed. "That answers that question. I'll put this on the table. Would you grab the salad out of the fridge?"

Allison pulled open the door of the well-stocked refrigerator, located the salad and carried it to the table.

"This is lovely," she said, assessing the glossy,

cherry wood tabletop set with deep-blue placemats, china and silverware. A fresh flower arrangement provided a centerpiece. "Fresh flowers? Did you bring them from the city?"

"No. I'm guessing that Mrs. Penny brought them when she stocked the refrigerator. She's a great cook, and when I explained that we were on our honeymoon, she insisted that she provide ready-to-heat meals for us as well as stock the pantry. She must have decided we needed flowers, too."

"They're beautiful."

The next hour flowed by so quickly that Allison forgot to worry about sharing a house and bed with Jorge. He told her interesting anecdotes about his life as a district attorney that fascinated and amused her, while she returned the favor with stories about law school classes and difficult professors that had him laughing with sympathy. After dinner they shared cleanup chores before wandering into the living room.

"Do you feel like watching a movie? Ross has a bookcase filled with titles from almost every genre." Jorge nodded at the small table in one corner. "Or we could play board games, if you like. Or," he looked at her and lifted a brow. "We could play cards?"

Allison pretended to consider his suggestions. "Hmm. I think I'd like to play cards."

"Good choice. You'll find several decks of cards

in the drawer in the game table. If you'll find a pack for us, I'll light the fire and we can sit in front of the hearth.''

"All right."

Jorge crossed the room and knelt in front of the fireplace to set a match to the kindling beneath the split wood. Allison realized that she was standing still, fascinated by the flexing and bunching of powerful thigh muscles as he bent one knee to lean forward and adjust a log. She shook herself and determinedly crossed to the small table, pulled open the shallow drawer beneath the parquet surface and found an unopened pack of cards.

By the time she reached the fireplace, flames were licking at the kindling and the bottoms of the logs, and Jorge had taken pillows from the sofa and tossed them on the floor.

"This is nice," Allison commented, dropping on to the thick oriental rug that covered the polished wooden floor in front of the raised stone hearth.

"Yeah, it is." Jorge stretched out on the floor, his stockinged feet near the hearth, his back against the sofa. "I've always liked this house. I haven't been up here with Ross and his family nearly as much as I'd like to in the past six months."

"Why not?" Allison asked, curious about his life.

"Too busy at work." He watched her hands as she broke the seal on the pack of cards, removed the jokers, then expertly shuffled the cards. "I'm guessing that you've played cards a few times in your life?"

She smiled, but managed to keep her voice free of gleeful anticipation. "A few times, yes."

One hour and several hands of poker later, Jorge eyed her threateningly, a reluctant smile curving his mouth. "You're a card shark, lady. Just where did you learn to play poker?"

"From my father and his friends. Dad hosts a Thursday-night poker group, and when I was little, I used to beg to sit on his lap and play his hand. He let me, until I was good enough that the others complained that we were winning all the pots. I think I was about ten years old at the time."

"A card shark at age ten? Geez," he groused, raising a brow and sighing as he picked up the cards she dealt him. "Did your dad teach you to cheat?"

"Absolutely not!" She was affronted.

"Then where did you learn?"

"From Uncle Roberto."

"Uncle Roberto? Was he a professional poker player?"

"No." She shook her head and laid down her hand. "Cards?"

"I'll stay with these."

"Dealer takes two." She discarded two cards on to the pile, then dealt herself two more before picking up her hand and frowning intensely as she quickly shifted the cards. "No, Uncle Roberto was a film director, but he said it was so boring to wait for actors to get into costume and makeup, that he learned to play poker in self-defense."

"A film director?" Jorge thought about the photos of her parents and the people with them in her office. His mouth opened, closed, then opened again. "Roberto Angelini? Is that the director who taught you to play poker?"

"Yes. But I always called him Uncle Roberto. He's my godfather." She looked up from her cards and found him staring at her. "What?"

"Roberto Angelini is your godfather?"

"Yes. Why, is that a problem?"

"No problem. I'm just a little amazed that you're so nonchalant about it."

"Why not?" She stared at him for a moment, puzzled, until enlightenment dawned. "Oh, you mean because he's *the* Roberto Angelini, the film director who won four Academy Awards in six years."

It wasn't a question; it was a statement.

"I suppose so. You have to admit, not many little ten-year-old girls are taught to cheat at poker by a world-famous film director."

Allison shrugged. "I don't think of him that way. To me, he was always Uncle Roberto, the man who always gave me a doll for my birthday and had peppermint candy in his coat pockets. And he liked my red hair.''

"Sounds like a nice guy." Jorge eyed her across the short span of carpet that separated their bodies. "And he had good taste. Who wouldn't like your hair?"

A stab of old pain hit Allison. "Just about everyone."

"Why?" he asked bluntly, his expression half frown, half bafflement.

"Because when I was a little girl, my hair was orangey-red, I had matching freckles everywhere, and I couldn't go out in the sun without burning a truly horrible lobster-red color. Red doesn't go well with carroty hair and freckles. I was every mother's nightmare—especially since we lived in California, among the tanned, blond, beautiful people.''

Jorge's deep chuckle stopped abruptly when she didn't smile back. "You aren't serious, are you?"

"I'm very serious."

He reached out and stroked his palm over the shiny fall of hair from the crown of her head to her chin, then curled a strand around his fingers, testing the silky texture against thumb and forefinger.

"You have the most beautiful hair I've ever seen. It's the first thing I noticed about you."

"Really?" Allison held her breath, the web of intimacy that spun between them taking all the oxygen from the air.

"Really. I looked across the ballroom and there you were, the light from the chandeliers pouring over you, your hair like a flame." His gaze left the strand of hair and met hers. "Then you turned around and I realized that the rest of you was just as beautiful." He frowned in consternation. "You're crying. Why are you crying?"

"Because no one's ever told me that before. You say the sweetest things."

"I told you before, I'm not sweet." His voice was huskier, edged with exasperation. "Just because I recognize a beautiful woman when I see one, doesn't mean I'm sweet." He bent his head and brushed a soft kiss against her mouth. "Sweet. That's as bad as hearing a woman say that she thinks of you as a brother."

Allison met his gaze. "I don't think of you as a brother," she whispered.

"Good." His eyes darkened, and his thumb moved over her bottom lip in slow, mesmerizing strokes. "Because I don't want to be your brother."

His mouth covered hers again, and Allison forgot about the cards in her hands and anything else but the sweet, hot slide of desire through her veins. He picked her up and settled her across his lap and she murmured in protest when he lifted his mouth from hers for a brief second. Then his fingers threaded through her hair, his hand cradled her head, and his mouth covered hers again with hot urgency.

Wrapped against the heated strength of his body, Allison quickly was swept up in passion. It wasn't until she felt cooler air against her midriff that she realized he'd unbuttoned her sweater. The chill was chased away by the warmth of his hand as he cupped one breast through her bra, his mouth hotter, more urgent on hers until he suddenly jerked away from her and stood.

Dazed, she lay where he left her on the carpet, staring up at him in confusion.

He thrust his hands through his hair and bit off a curse. "I'm sorry," he muttered. "I didn't mean to let things get out of hand. I know you need time to adjust to being married, and I swore I'd give it to you." He caught her hands and pulled her to her feet. "Why don't you have a shower and get your pajamas on while I warm a glass of milk."

And before Allison had time to adjust to the sudden switch from passion to warm milk, he hustled her down the hallway and was closing the door behind him as he left the bedroom. She stood, staring at the door panels for a long moment before she shook her head and took a black lace slip nightgown from the dresser drawer and went to the bathroom.

Moments later, shower finished, teeth and hair brushed, wearing the thigh-length black slip that was a wedding gift from Zoe, she padded barefoot back into the bedroom and stopped abruptly when she saw Jorge.

He stood beside the bed, the blankets turned down, plumping the pillows.

"You don't really expect me to drink that, do you?"

He looked over his shoulder and went perfectly still, his eyes going black with heat as his gaze ran swiftly over her from head to toe. Slowly he straightened.

Allison's legs trembled at the promise in those dark eyes, at the swift clenching of his hands at his sides and the ripple of chest and shoulder muscles beneath the white T-shirt as he checked himself.

"Drink what?" His voice was distracted, rough and the slightest bit unsteady.

"The warm milk." Allison walked to the bed, her bare arm brushing his chest as she reached the nightstand and picked up the glass. She wrinkled her nose in distaste and looked up at him through her lashes. His eyes were hot, predatory, his body taut. "I really don't like warm milk."

"Okay." A muscle flexed in his jaw. "I'll take the glass away. Get in bed." He held the blanket and sheet back.

Allison sat on the edge of the bed, feeling the heat like a brand on her skin as his gaze followed the movement of her legs when she lifted them onto the bed and lay down. He didn't say a word, only tucked the blankets around her waist before he planted his fists on each side of her and bent to brush a chaste kiss on her brow. "Good night." The word was guttural, his voice a deep growl.

"Good night, Jorge."

With one last, blistering look, he turned and strode out of the room, snapping off the light as he went and closing the door behind him.

"This is my wedding night," she said aloud, staring at the ceiling in frustration. "And I'm in bed, alone."

Was Jorge no longer interested in making love with her now that she was pregnant? He'd certainly seemed interested earlier, when he'd kissed her in front of the fireplace. He'd said he didn't want to be her brother, so why was he treating her as if she were untouchable? Okay, so she had to admit that sharing space with a male was a little intimidating. She'd lived alone since leaving her parents' home, and even as a child, she'd been a solitary soul.

Maybe I'm too reserved and he thinks I don't want him. The thought of making a blatant sexual overture to Jorge was overwhelming; she painfully admitted that she was too unsure of herself to risk rejection. Just stripping down and taking a shower while knowing he was in the next room was intimidating.

Still, how was she to become accustomed to living with her husband if they didn't share a bed?

Frustrated with her inability to understand the mixed signals she was getting from Jorge and from the arousal that still heated her blood, Allison slammed her eyes shut and ordered her wayward thoughts to cease. When she finally fell asleep, she tossed and turned, restless with dreams.

Jorge paced the living room and swore silently. He'd promised himself that after rushing Allison into marriage and gently bullying her into agreeing to move in with him, he wouldn't pressure her to make love. But every instinct he owned was urging him to claim her.

He groaned aloud and stopped pacing to stare out the window at the dark woods outside. For the first time, it occurred to him to wonder if he was making a mistake in not using their physical bond to strengthen the marriage against the other problems that lay between them. They hadn't spent a lot of time together, and although Jorge was convinced beyond any doubt that Allison was the one woman in the world meant for him, he didn't blame her for being wary and concerned about giving up her independence and moving in with a man she hardly knew.

Am I rationalizing because I want her so badly? He stared out the window, his face grim. Unfortunately, the thought processes that he used with incisive clarity in the courtroom didn't help him now.

His ability to reason was too impacted by the lust and need that pounded through his veins. *It would help if she didn't want me as badly,* he thought. Every time he touched her, they both went up in flames. He thrust his fingers through his hair and went back to pacing the floor.

It took an hour of pacing, worrying, examining his motivation and considering what was ultimately best for their marriage before Jorge finally decided that their marriage needed all the help it could get and that the physical bond held the best prospect of strengthening their emotional bond. He'd woo her with care and consideration by day and take advantage of the heat between them at night. He still wasn't sure that his decision wasn't influenced by lust, but he was beyond caring.

He slipped quietly into the darkened bedroom. The bedclothes were tumbled, one of the pillows tossed on the floor. Jorge picked up the pillow and returned it to the bed, then stripped down to his boxers and slid beneath the blankets with Allison. She muttered, the words incomprehensible, and twisted against the pillow, rolling on to her side with her back to him, her restless movements further tangling the blankets.

Jorge slipped an arm around her waist and eased her against him, curving his body against the soft, warm shape of hers. She sighed, snuggled closer and relaxed, falling deeper into sleep.

He nearly groaned aloud when she cuddled against him, the round curve of her bottom nestling against his groin. His palm lay over her stomach, and he thought he felt a small outward curve that might be the baby. Lust still throbbed and ached, but he felt immeasurably calmer and content with Allison in his arms, and despite his assumption that he would lie awake unsatisfied and frustrated, he soon fell asleep.

Allison woke slowly. Warm and comfortable, she put off opening her eyes as she drifted upward from a happy, hazy dream that she only faintly remembered.

She was cradled in warmth along her back. She stretched lazily, her toes brushing other feet, and she froze, eyes opening wide. Carefully she turned her head on the pillow to find Jorge watching her, his eyes lazy, heat kindling with each move of her body against his.

"Good morning." His voice was husky.

"Good morning," she managed to get out. "What are you doing here?"

"Sleeping—and waiting for you to wake up. How about you?"

"How about me...what?"

"Were you waiting for me?" He pressed a kiss against the soft skin of her shoulder, and she shivered, goose bumps pebbling her skin in reaction to his touch.

"To wake up?"

He trailed his fingers over the curve of her stomach, then settled his warm palm there, his hand big enough to span her abdomen, his fingers and thumb touching her hip bones. "Yeah. Or...whatever."

"Whatever?" Her voice was throaty, her thoughts scattered, and she was unable to concentrate on a rational reply as he smoothed the black satin over her skin. His arm tightened and he pressed closer, his thighs rock hard behind hers, her bottom pressed tighter against his hips. He shifted against her, and she caught her breath. He was fully aroused.

"Jorge," she said weakly, her eyes drifting half closed as his mouth brushed against her nape and he nipped the soft skin there. Desire surged and she struggled to maintain her sanity. "Jorge, I think we should talk about this."

"What's there to talk about?" He rolled her to her back and rose above her, brushed kisses against her eyebrows and the line of her cheekbones. His voice was shades deeper than normal, husky with emotion. "I want you. You want me. We're married. This is perfectly legal and we've got a wedding certificate to prove it."

"I know, but..."

"Shhh." He slipped the narrow black satin strap off one shoulder and replaced it with his open mouth, his tongue stroking against her sensitive skin. The cool silk of his hair brushed against her throat. "We're good together, Allison. I must have been insane to let you fall asleep alone last night."

Then his mouth covered hers, his tongue thrust, rough velvet against hers, and she forgot whatever it was that she'd meant to ask him.

His mouth moved lower, nudging the black satin away from her breast until his lips found the tightly ruched nipple. When he drew it into his mouth and sucked, Allison's hips came off the bed and she wrapped her arms around his neck, surging upward against the hard length of his body.

"Yes," he whispered, pressing her back against the sheets, his hips settling against hers. When she instinctively shifted to make a place for him and wrapped her legs around his waist, he groaned, surging against her. He smoothed one hand down the fragile satin that separated her from him and lifted his head, his mouth taking hers as he joined them with one powerful thrust. Allison gasped, her body going taut as she struggled to adjust, her nails scoring half-moons on the powerful muscles of his biceps.

He didn't move. His much bigger body hung over her slender frame, supported by his forearms, trembling with the effort.

"Are you okay?" The words were guttural, his voice thick.

The sensation of being impaled eased and Allison

nodded, her gaze fastened on his face, his features
harsh, the bones sharp with desire. She lifted her
arms, wrapping them around his neck, and tugged
his mouth down to meet hers. His harsh groan was
the only sound in the quiet room as he drove them
both to the edge and sent them crashing over.

By the time the weekend was over, Allison was
totally confused and had no clear idea as to the
relationship between herself and her new husband.
He was solicitous and kind during the day, always
asking after her health and the baby, but he treated
her as if he were a caring, affectionate brother. No
more hot looks and slow kisses. At least, not during
the day. But when the lights went out and they were
in bed together, the passion that was never far from
the surface exploded between them.

But each morning when they rose, Jorge went
back to being the kind, considerate, concerned man
whose touch was impersonal, whose glances were
affectionate but not passionate.

Allison had no idea what was going on between
them. He obviously enjoyed making love with her.
Even her limited experience convinced her that he
loved what they did together when they went to
bed. But his distance during the day convinced her
that the lovemaking that shook her to the core was
only convenient sex for him. She teetered between
hope and happiness, despair and worry. Horribly

unsure of herself, and of Jorge, she retreated behind a wall of cool politeness, unable to tell him her fears and her growing wish that their marriage could be a real one.

For his part Jorge wasn't sure his plan was working. At night she was the passionate woman he'd wanted back in his bed. He couldn't get enough of her, nor she of him, but during the day she seemed to retreat behind a wall. She never voluntarily touched him or sought him out, and his impatient nature urged him to back her up against a wall and demand that she tell him what she was thinking behind her cool amber eyes and polite smiles. He considered keeping her in bed both day and night, but the pregnancy manuals he'd read hadn't addressed whether a newly pregnant woman could safely indulge in twenty-four-hour-a-day lovemaking. So he gritted his teeth, struggled to keep his hands off Allison during daylight hours and continued to try to court her with affection and kindness while he waited impatiently for the night to come.

The drive back to New York was quiet. Jorge had a wide selection of music to choose from and they took turns picking CDs, amiably arguing over the merits of rock, blues and classical artists as they listened. It was just before lunchtime when they arrived at Jorge's apartment building.

He swung the Jag into the underground car park below the building, and they rode the elevator to the nineteenth floor. Her arms full of shopping bags, Allison waited silently while Jorge unlocked the door and stood back to let her enter the apartment.

Despite knowing that Zoe had coordinated with the moving company who had emptied her apartment, transferred her belongings and unpacked for her, Allison was still taken aback to find her framed print of Monet's water lilies hanging on the entryway wall.

"I asked Zoe to supervise the movers, but I didn't realize that she was going to move me in so completely. We can take the print down."

"No, let's leave it." He closed the door and paused, eyeing the print. "I like it. I've never bothered to do much with this apartment except stack books and files on the furniture. It's nice to see something on the wall." He gestured toward the living room, their traveling bags in both hands and one tucked under his arm. "Let's see what else Zoe did."

Allison had arranged to have most of her furniture given away or sold and had only kept a few pieces. The silver-framed photos of her family were grouped on a shelf of the large entertainment center, along with a small collection of antique salt and pepper shakers. The huge Boston fern that had held center stage in her small living room now resided in one corner of Jorge's much larger space, close enough to receive indirect sunlight from the big window, far enough away not to sunburn the delicate fronds. On the wall behind the fern hung her print of an 1898 Paris musical revue with cancan dancers, the deep reds and blues held in a simple gold frame. The dark-blue afghan she'd knitted in college was folded across the back of the leather sofa, and the wicker basket of knitting wool and needles that she hadn't had time to touch in simply ages sat nearby.

"Nice." Jorge's voice held satisfaction.

"You don't mind?"

"No—I told you, it's nice to see the apartment looking more like a home and less like a neglected office space."

He turned and led the way down the hall. Allison followed him, and when she entered the bedroom, he was dropping his bags at the end of the bed, then he swung hers atop the spread.

"I emptied half the dresser drawers for you and half the closet space." He crossed the room and slid back the mirrored doors.

Zoe had clearly been busy here also, for Allison's shoes were neatly lined up on the closet floor, and suits, blouses and dresses hung on the pole.

"Looks like Zoe unpacked for you," he commented, flicking a glance over the interior before turned to Allison. "Remind me to thank her. I'm guessing that the less time you spend unpacking the better for you and the baby, right?"

"Yes." Allison's gaze moved over the room. Her antique wicker table served as a nightstand on the far side of the bed, her reading lamp, alarm clock, a biography of Thomas Jefferson and a novel by her favorite mystery author were arranged neatly on the glass top. She walked to the bathroom and peered in. The room had a huge walk-in shower and a large, jetted bathtub. Her collection of perfume bottles was neatly arranged in one corner of the marble-topped vanity. The evidence of the huge change in her life was suddenly overwhelming and panicked, she glanced over her shoulder to find Jorge watching her, his dark gaze unreadable.

"It's almost lunchtime, are you hungry?"

His calm reference to ordinary life steadied her, and she nodded, suddenly realizing that her stomach felt hollow. "I am. As a matter of fact I'm starved." She glanced down at her midsection, still flat beneath the yellow sweater she wore. "I can't believe how hungry I am, all the time. Either this child is going to be born full-size, or we have a potential fullback on our hands."

Jorge laughed. "Good, he can grow up, play pro ball and keep his poor parents in style." He strode across the room, slung an arm around Allison's shoulders and urged her out the door. "Let's see what we have in the refrigerator for lunch."

The following morning Allison paused outside the main doors to Manhattan Multiples and drew a deep breath, steeling herself before going inside.

"Good morning, Josie."

The receptionist looked up when the door opened and smiled, her bright-blue eyes sparkling with warmth. "Good morning, Allison. How was your long weekend?"

"Great." Allison nodded. Should she tell Josie she'd gotten married? No, better to tell Eloise first, then everyone else. "And how was your weekend?"

"Excellent." Josie gathered a handful of messages from Allison's slot and handed them to her. "I read a new poem at The Inside Out's open-mike night on Saturday, and the audience loved it."

"That's wonderful." Allison smiled with genuine delight as she took the pink message slips. Josie's poetry was her passion, and it was impossible not to feel the joy that vibrated from her when her work was appreciated.

When the phone rang, Josie took the call, waggling her fingers in silent response to Allison's goodbye.

Allison entered her office, flipped on the light switch, dropped her briefcase, message slips and purse on top of the desk and shrugged out of her coat. She hung it on a hook of the coat tree in the corner and returned to her desk where she tucked her purse into a drawer, shifted her briefcase to the floor and quickly scanned the phone messages. Satisfied that nothing in the notes required her immediate attention, she eyed the overflowing in-box on the corner of her desk and, with a sigh, removed the first file and opened it.

An hour later, having dealt with the urgent matters in the pile of work accumulated over the short time she'd been out of the office, Allison drew a deep breath and resolutely left her office to find Eloise.

Fortunately for her nerves, Eloise was easily located in her office. Allison tapped on the open door, and her boss glanced up, a smile breaking over her face.

"Allison. Come in. How was your holiday? I hope you're going to tell me that you had an absolutely decadent, wonderful time so I can live vicariously through you, because I worked all weekend."

"You worked all weekend?" Allison stepped across the threshold and closed the door before walking across the thick carpet to the row of chairs in front of Eloise's desk. She dropped into one and eyed her boss with concern. "Why did you have to work this weekend? Was it something I could have helped you with? I wouldn't have gone out of town if I'd known you needed me."

"I was crunching numbers for the consultant who's working on a plan to apply for federal grant funding. And although I'm sure you would have been an immense help, I would never have wanted you to cancel your weekend. You haven't taken a day off in ages. Speaking of which,'' Eloise picked up her coffee mug and sipped, her eyes twinkling with interest as she eyed Allison over the rim. ''Tell me what you did this weekend? Did you have fun?''

''Umm, yes,'' Allison said, her words stilted. How was she going to say this? She decided to simply say the words. ''I was married on Thursday, and we left the city over the weekend for our honeymoon.''

Eloise's eyes rounded. She stared at Allison as if she'd just announced that she'd spent the weekend on the moon.

Chapter Seven

"You were married? You spent the weekend on your honeymoon?" Eloise repeated the words, her disbelief evident in the tone.

"Yes."

Eloise blinked slowly, clearly stunned by Allison's bombshell. "How did I miss this? I didn't even know that you were dating someone, let alone considering marriage."

"It was a whirlwind courtship." The lie fell easily from her lips, but Allison was flooded with guilt.

"Who is he?"

"His name is Jorge Perez."

Eloise sat bolt upright, her coffee forgotten, her

eyes wide. "Jorge Perez? Are we talking about Assistant District Attorney, Jorge Perez?"

"Yes."

"Good heavens, Allison. The man's practically a celebrity. Wherever did you meet him?"

"At a fund-raiser we both attended a couple of months ago. A save-the-whales group organized the function, wonderful food, and the ballroom was decorated in a deep-sea theme, quite beautiful, really. There were professors stationed at intervals around the room, lecturing and answering questions, very clever idea." Allison realized she was chattering and abruptly stopped talking. Eloise was eyeing her strangely.

"I see. And you met Jorge at this fund-raiser—through mutual friends, perhaps?"

"No. We sort of, well…" Allison smiled as she remembered. "We discovered that we have a mutual interest in astronomy."

Eloise blinked. "Astronomy?"

"Yes, astronomy."

"I wasn't aware that you were interested in either astronomy or saving whales from extinction," Eloise murmured. "So you've known him only two months and you decided to elope?"

"Yes."

"Extraordinary. Forgive me, Allison, but this is difficult to take in. It's not like you to be so impulsive. Now if it were Josie telling me this, well, that would be perfectly understandable. But you...you're just not—'' Eloise lifted one hand in a gesture of confusion.

''Romantic?'' Allison offered, scrambling to come up with an explanation that Eloise would accept. She wasn't ready to confess it was her pregnancy that had prompted the marriage. She needed to believe there were other compelling reasons, such as a growing bond between her and Jorge. Settling for a portion of the truth, she said, ''He swept me off my feet, Eloise. I've never met anyone like him before. He's...amazing.''

Eloise's worried gaze softened as Allison spoke. ''Forgive me for being so surprised, Allison. Of course he's amazing and wonderful, otherwise you would never have married him.'' The phone on her desk buzzed. ''Excuse me just one second.'' She lifted the receiver. ''Yes? All right. Just a moment.'' She covered the mouthpiece with one hand. ''I'm sorry, Allison, I have to take this call. But we must celebrate your wonderful news.''

''We will.'' Relieved to have escaped with relative ease, Allison slipped out of the office, leaving Eloise absorbed in her phone call, and returned to her desk.

For the next hour the staff of Manhattan Multiples popped into Allison's office to voice their congratulations, their reactions much like Eloise's— surprise, shock and delight. Despite their friendly interest, however, Allison sensed a definite undercurrent of disbelief when she repeated her story that she and Jorge were wildly in love and had a whirlwind affair that culminated in marriage. None of them voiced it, however, until Josie appeared in her doorway, paused to peer up and down the hall before closing the door with a snap, then marched across the room to plop into a chair.

"Okay, give," she demanded, leaning forward, elbows on her knees, her gaze fastened on Allison. "Tell me everything. And not that version you gave the rest of the office, I want the real scoop."

"I have no idea what you're talking about," Allison replied, carefully slotting a graph chart into an employee's file.

"I mean the true story about you and the gorgeous Assistant District Attorney. Where did you meet him?"

"At a fund-raiser to raise money for an organization committed to saving whales." Allison had repeated the line so many times that she thought her voice was beginning to sound robotic.

"Are you sure?" Josie said suspiciously. "He didn't arrest you for speeding or something, did he?"

Startled, Allison laughed out loud at the intrigued expression on Josie's face. "No, he definitely did not. And even if I had a car to speed in, which I haven't, I don't think assistant district attorneys arrest people, Josie, they just prosecute them after the police arrest them.''

''Oh.'' Josie frowned in thought, pursing her lips as she eyed Allison. ''It seems very strange to me that you haven't mentioned this guy, not even once, over the past couple of months. Leah saw him when he came to the office a week or so ago, and she says he's gorgeous. How could you keep quiet for two whole months about being involved in a mad, passionate affair with a well-known, handsome hunk like Jorge Perez?''

''I'm a pretty quiet person,'' Allison said wryly. ''Haven't you noticed?''

''Yes, but Jorge Perez isn't. Which makes me wonder why news of you two dating wasn't mentioned in the papers.''

''I don't know, but I'm glad it wasn't.'' Allison didn't have to fake her fervent response. She was having enough trouble coping with her relationship with Jorge in private; she definitely didn't want gossip columnists speculating about them.

''That would make you uncomfortable, wouldn't it?'' Josie's quick concern was sincere. ''Should I tell the rest of the staff not to mention your big news outside the office?''

''I'd appreciate it if you would, Josie,'' Allison managed a smile. ''I admit I hadn't thought about that aspect of marrying someone as well-known as

Jorge and frankly, I'm not sure I'm ready to handle questions from reporters.''

"Don't worry, I'll pass the word." Josie glanced at her watch and rose from her chair with quick grace. "Yikes, I was supposed to have last year's budget projections copied and on Eloise's desk five minutes ago." And with a quick goodbye, she whisked out of the office.

Allison felt as if she'd been hit by a whirlwind. Why hadn't she considered that the press might be interested in Jorge's marriage? He was a prominent member of the legal community and currently involved in several high-profile cases.

She hated dealing with reporters. They brought back memories of too many crowd scenes with her parents when she was a child. The confusion and fear she'd felt when surrounded by camera flashes and shouted questions, the chaos of the crowd as her parents and she were hustled from building to car, were all part of celebrity life that she'd grown to dislike intensely.

But Jorge isn't part of a profession that courts the press, she reminded herself. His work generated interest among the media because of the human interest element, but he didn't personally chase headlines. Their conversations about the ups and downs of being a career district attorney had reassured her on that point.

Determined not to worry about what, if any, interest the press might have in her marriage, Allison forced her attention back to the stack of work on her desk.

Later that evening after sharing a late, post-class dinner with Jorge and they were preparing for bed, Allison broached the subject.

"Jorge, someone at the office made a comment today that had me wondering—do you expect reporters to take an interest in our wedding?"

Already showered and in bed, the sheets pulled to his waist, Jorge put down the book he'd been reading while he waited for her. "Are you worried that they might?" he asked quietly.

"Not worried, exactly." She slid open the closet doors, hung her suit inside and closed the doors, before crossing to the bed. He pulled back the blankets and she sat cross-legged on the bed, a faint frown veeing her brows while she squirted lotion into her palm and smoothed the fragrant cream over her hands. "I'm not really comfortable dealing with the media," she confessed.

"Then I'll handle any questions that come up." He smoothed his hand over her bent knee, his fingers splaying over her thigh. "Anything else bothering you?"

She glanced sideways at him, her pulse already quickening at the touch of his hand and the sound of his roughened voice.

"No," she murmured. "Nothing."

"Good." He tumbled her on to the pillows, his muscled body a warm, welcome weight.

At least this part of their marriage seemed to work, she thought hazily, before passion pulled her under.

Between the upcoming criminal trial that Jorge was involved in, Allison's schedule at Manhattan Multiples, her night classes, and her pregnancy-induced weariness, the newly wedded couple found little spare time to work on their marriage. Sometimes Allison felt as if the only time she felt truly married to Jorge was when they were making love. During those moments she felt connected and sure of him. She was gradually growing accustomed to the novelty of sharing a bathroom, his aftershave mingling with the scent of her perfume, their towels hanging side by side on the bar.

Two weeks after their wedding, Jorge called to tell her that he had to work late at the office and didn't know what time he'd be home. Allison ate dinner early and though it was barely 7:00 p.m., headed for the shower. A half hour later, her makeup scrubbed off, flannel pajama bottoms paired with a cropped T-shirt keeping her warm, she turned on CNN without the sound and settled on to the sofa to study.

She'd hardly completed her notes on the first three pages of assigned reading for the following

Monday night's class when the doorbell rang. Wondering if Jorge had forgotten his key and had come home early, she shuffled the books, paper and pens off her lap and on to the sofa's broad cushion and hurried to the door.

But it wasn't Jorge she saw when she peered through the peephole in the door, it was an older, dark-haired woman. She glanced down at her pajamas, shrugged and slipped the locks free to open the door.

"Hello?" she inquired, curious at the swift, assessing glance the woman gave her.

"Hello. You must be Allison?"

"Yes."

"I'm Jorge's mother, Benita."

Allison's eyes widened. Stunned, she could only stare.

"May I come in?"

"Yes. Of course." Galvanized, Allison immediately stepped back, opening the door wide. "Please do."

The attractive older woman, silver glinting in her short black hair, stepped into the apartment and glanced past Allison into the living room. "Is Jorge home?"

"No. I'm sorry, he's not. He had to work late at the office." Allison closed the door and caught a glimpse of herself in the entry mirror. She nearly groaned aloud. The light-blue flannel pajama bottoms were patterned with penguins, her feet were bare, her hair ruffled from her absentminded habit of pushing her pencil through it, and she wasn't wearing a speck of makeup. In contrast, Benita Perez was impeccably dressed in a wool herringbone pantsuit with a white turtleneck beneath the neat jacket and stylish black boots. Small gold hoop earrings gleamed against her black hair, and the black bag slung over her shoulder matched the expensive leather of her boots.

"I returned home from a trip to visit my sister-in-law in Florida and learned from my niece, Rita, that Jorge was married while I was away."

"Yes. Judge Maddock married us. It was quite sudden. I'm sure Jorge would have told you, but you were out of town and..." Allison's voice trailed off uneasily under Benita's shrewd gaze. "I'm sorry. We should have waited until you were home and could come to the ceremony. I didn't think...my parents wouldn't have cared and it didn't occur to me that you might..." She stopped speaking, helpless to know how to explain an oversight that now seemed to be enormously rude and unforgivably unfeeling. "I don't know how I could have been so inconsiderate," she muttered, pushing her fingers through her hair in distraction.

Benita's expression softened. "It wasn't your fault, dear. Jorge should have called me." Her eyes narrowed consideringly. "And since he didn't, I can only assume that there's something about this marriage that he didn't want me to know.''

Horrified, Allison felt cold dread spread from her toes to her fingers.

"And now that I've seen you, I'm sure I know what that something is," Benita smiled, the quirk of her lips delighted. "It was love at first sight, wasn't it?"

"Umm…" Allison didn't know what to say.

"I always told him that he'd meet the right woman and fall head over heels in love, just like his father and I did. And he always swore that he was much too practical to choose a wife in such an illogical way. I'm sure he's putting off telling me because he'll have to confess that he's just like his romantic-minded parents.'' Benita laughed and swept Allison into a warm hug. "Tell me all about how you and my son met."

"Of course." Allison managed to gather her wits. "Let's make a pot of tea and I'll tell you everything." Thank goodness she'd already prepared a story to explain her wedding to her co-workers.

A half hour later, the two women sat in the living room, comfortably settled on the leather sofa, and sipped herbal tea.

"Do you have a lot of family in Florida?" Allison asked politely.

"My husband's sister and two brothers have retired there.'' Benita paused, contemplated her tea-cup for a moment, then glanced at Allison. "I don't know if Jorge told you, but we lost his father when he was quite young.''

"Yes, I know. He told me about the shooting. It must have been terrible for a child his age to see, and how awful for you to lose your husband to such senseless violence.''

Benita nodded. "It was a horrible time in our lives. Losing his father had a huge impact on Jorge. He went from being a fun-loving little boy to a serious young man committed to preventing violence.'' Her gaze warmed and she covered Allison's hand with hers. "Jorge never talks about that day, not even to me.''

Allison didn't know what to say. The magic of that night had seemed to erase all the normal barriers between them, making them confidants instead of strangers. She'd told Jorge about her inability to feel close to her parents, her fierce determination to use a law degree to make a difference in the world, and a dozen other things that she never discussed with anyone else. She hadn't realized that he'd done the same. "Then, perhaps it's good that he was able to talk to me about it,'' she said finally, aware that Benita expected a response.

"I'm sure it is. I can't tell you how happy I am that Jorge has found you,'' Benita confided. "I must say that I never cared for Celeste and was relieved when she broke off the engagement.''

"Jorge was engaged to be married? Recently?'' Allison's heart clenched at the thought that Jorge had been engaged to someone else, loved someone else. *But he doesn't love me.* The thought only made her chest ache more.

"Not recently, no. It was a couple of years ago,'' Benita assured her. "To a young woman from a socially prominent family. I believe they met through her grandfather, who's a judge on the appellate court. I'm sure she would have been an asset to his career, she certainly had all the right connections,'' Benita said thoughtfully. "But I felt she was all wrong for him in all the ways that truly matter. She was very involved in a number of organizations and was forever dragging Jorge to one dinner and ballroom gala or another. Not that there's anything wrong with being socially active,'' she assured Allison. "But Celeste wanted Jorge to accompany her to social events nearly every night of the week. I doubt they ever spent a quiet night at home the entire time they dated. I know my son too well to believe that a life spent partying would have made him happy. I wasn't surprised when the engagement was called off. I had the impression that Jorge's heart wasn't involved.'' She smiled at Allison and abruptly changed the subject. "It's lovely that you plan to become an attorney, too, what a great deal the two of you must have in common.''

More than you know, Allison thought, but she didn't voice it. ''Yes, we're both intrigued by the practice of law. I think it's good to have careers in common.''

''Absolutely. Have the two of you discussed children?'' Benita immediately clapped her hand over her mouth, her dark eyes guilty. ''Oh, my goodness. I can't believe I said that. I always swore that when Jorge married, I wouldn't be an interfering mother-in-law. But all my sisters have grandchildren, and I must confess I was beginning to wonder if Jorge was ever going to get married and have babies.''

Benita looked so much like a child caught with her fingers in the cookie jar that Allison couldn't take offense. Instead, she burst out laughing. ''I'm sure it's a perfectly natural thing to wonder about. And yes,'' she added solemnly, ''we have discussed children.''

''Oh, good,'' Benita said fervently. Her eyes twinkled. ''And I won't ask you when, but just so you know—I'm ready to baby-sit anytime you need me!''

''Good to know,'' Allison assured her, returning her warm smile.

''Since you're an only child, like Jorge,'' Benita commented, ''I'm guessing that I'll have to draw straws with your parents to decide who gets to baby-sit first.''

"Mmm-hmm." Allison sipped her tea, her response as noncommittal as possible without revealing that she doubted her parents would be fascinated by her child. They were sure to send an expensive christening gift, but whether they'd be anxious to spend time with their grandchild was doubtful. Their lives were far too busy.

"I must be going, I've kept you from studying long enough." Benita leaned forward to return her teacup to the tray on the coffee table, collected her purse and rose.

Allison stood and walked with her to the door.

"I know Jorge will be so sorry that he missed your visit," she said as she opened the door.

"Tell him that I'm sorry I missed him, as well, but it gave us a chance to get acquainted, which was lovely." Benita smiled, her dark eyes so like Jorge's. "I'm very glad that he's found you, Allison. I was afraid that he'd chosen another heartless social butterfly like the ones he's dated in the past, but it's very clear that you aren't like that at all." She enclosed Allison in a quick hug and a drift of faint perfume. "Tell that son of mine to call me—and we'll set a date for you and Jorge to come out to the house for dinner."

"I'd like that." Allison waved goodbye and closed the door, leaning against it and feeling a bit as if she'd been caught up in a whirlwind. Jorge's mother was charming, and as intense and quick-witted as her son. In the short hour they'd spent together, Benita had managed to learn most of the basic details of Allison's life, except the fact that she was already pregnant. Allison had the uneasy feeling that it would be a serious mistake to try to fool her for long as to the real reasons she and Jorge had married.

She returned to her studying and became so absorbed in the work that it wasn't until she heard Jorge's key in the lock that she glanced at the digital clock on the stereo and realized that it was after 11:00 p.m.

She turned to look over the back of the sofa and saw him pause in the entryway to shrug out of his coat and hang it in the closet.

"Hi."

"Hi, yourself." He walked into the living room and sat on the ottoman, facing her, a smile tilting his lips, his eyes warm as he searched her face. "What are you doing up so late? I thought you'd be sound asleep when I got home."

Allison's heart caught, and she couldn't help returning his smile. "I lost track of time."

"What are you studying?" He leaned forward and picked up the book lying open on her lap. "*Kelly v. The State of New York?*"

"I'm researching cases supporting the right of a student to sue the school board."

"Ah." He grinned and returned the book to her lap. "What did you eat for dinner?"

She wrinkled her nose at him. "A very healthy, grilled chicken breast, green beans and a salad. And yes," she said to forestall him, "before you ask, I drank milk."

"Good."

"I feel like I'm living with the nutrition police," she complained, smiling when he laughed. She loved his laugh. Deep and throaty. His eyes crinkled at the corners when he was amused. His laughter eased the tension from his shoulders and face, caused by a long day in court. "I had a visitor tonight."

"Really? Who?" He tugged his tie free and unbuttoned the top four buttons of his shirt, visibly relaxing.

"Your mother."

His jaw dropped, then he groaned and rolled his eyes. "Damn. She's home already? She wasn't due back for another week."

"She said to tell you to call her. I got the definite impression that you're in big trouble because you didn't tell her we were getting married."

He groaned again and raked his fingers through his hair, ruffling the silky black strands. "I wanted to tell her in person, not over the telephone. What else did she say?''

Allison found it endearing that Jorge, over six feet and a powerfully muscled two hundred plus pounds, was clearly worried that his tiny dynamo of a mother was upset with him. ''She wanted to know if we've discussed children.''

He visibly tensed. ''And what did you tell her?''

''I assured her that we've discussed the subject.''

''You didn't tell her that you're pregnant?''

''No. I didn't know what you wanted to tell her about the baby, or when.''

''To tell you the truth, I haven't had time to decide what to tell her and I haven't had time to discuss it with you, in case you had any concerns.'' His gaze held hers. ''Were you okay with her asking you about our plans?''

''Yes, I think it's nice to know that our baby will have a grandmother eagerly waiting to hold her. She told me that she wanted to volunteer for baby-sitting.''

''That's my mom. She loves kids. Too bad she only had me.''

''She didn't remarry after your father died?''

''No. She said that marrying someone else would be settling for second best, and a husband didn't deserve that.''

The handsome lines of his face were relaxed, warm with affection.

"It's so nice that you and your mother are close," she said, resisting the urge to lean closer and brush the fall of black hair off his brow.

"For a long time it was just her and me against the world," he commented. "She went to work as a secretary after Dad died, and saved every penny she could squeeze out of the budget to put in a college fund for me. I was determined to be an attorney, and she was just as determined as I was that I'd succeed."

"Who cared for you while she worked?" Allison was fascinated by this glimpse into his childhood, so different from hers.

"A collection of aunts and cousins." He grinned at her. "I'm an only child, but Dad and Mom both come from huge families. Dad had three brothers and two sisters, and Mom has five brothers and one sister. All of them married and produced big families so I have cousins by the dozens. It's not just my mother who'll demand an explanation as to why we didn't have a huge wedding, the whole family will gather to rake me over the coals."

"Oh, my goodness," Allison said faintly. "I had no idea."

"I know. I should have told you before, but to tell you the truth, I didn't think about it. I expected Mom to be home next week, and I'd planned to take you to meet her then. Did she say who told her that we were married?"

"I think she said that it was Rita."

"I should have known. Rita is the designated gossip-central on Dad's side of the family. When we were kids, we used to say that there were two ways to make something public, tell the *New York Times,* or tell Rita."

Jorge's gaze softened as Allison laughed, and he cupped her chin, smoothing his thumb against the curve of her cheek. "Are you okay with this?"

"With what?"

"With a very large, noisy and very nosy family. I know you grew up in a quieter home with a much smaller family. The Perezes and Sanchezes together can be overwhelming when you're not used to them, but they mean well."

"Then I'm sure I'll adjust. I'm looking forward to meeting them, especially since they sound like a wonderful contrast to my parents, whose work schedules won't allow them to fly to New York and grill us about marrying for at least another month."

"Have you heard from them?"

"No." Allison had called her parents to tell them she was married, but they were out of the country, exploring filming sites in Thailand for their next project, and she'd had to leave a message with the housekeeper. Jorge had seemed surprised that she didn't try to locate them, and she hadn't wanted to confess that they were unlikely to cancel their trip and hurry to New York to meet her new husband.

Their casual level of interest in her life was a sharp contrast to Benita's concern for her son.

He leaned closer and kissed her, his mouth gentle. When he lifted his head, they were both breathing faster, the desire that was never far from the surface palpable between them.

"It's late. Let's go to bed."

Allison put her hand in his and let him draw her to her feet and down the hall to the bedroom.

Jorge scanned the morning paper while he ate breakfast and watched his wife as she read her own sections.

She sat across from him at the breakfast bar in the kitchen, her hair smooth and glossy, makeup discreetly applied. The tailored jacket of her caramel-colored wool suit hung on the back of her chair, leaving her in a long-sleeved, white silk blouse tucked into a knee-length, narrow skirt. Jorge would have bet his next paycheck that she thought the blouse, primly buttoned to just below her throat, was proper and completely nonsexy. If she knew how badly he wanted to unbutton the row of buttons that marched from the soft hollow of her throat to her waist, drawing the eye to the full curves of her breasts, she would likely have a heart attack. Just thinking about spreading open the unbuttoned silk and running his mouth over her soft, silky skin made him hard.

She sipped herbal tea from a gently steaming cup and nibbled toast with marmalade. He wanted to lean over and lick the tiny spot of orange marmalade from the corner of her mouth.

Instead, he was forced to watch the pink tip of her tongue follow the curve of her bottom lip and whisk it away.

He dragged his gaze away from the erotic sight and tried to focus on the paper. It was several moments before he actually saw the black print and not a replay of her mouth and tongue.

"Why don't you come to court with me and sit in on the trial this morning?" he asked, returning to their earlier discussion about the murder trial he was currently trying. Her thoughtful questions regarding his approach to a hostile defense witness had given him new insight. "I'm cross-examining Jackson this morning."

Allison looked up, her gaze surprised and pleased. "I'd love to." Her smile faded and she frowned. "But I have to stop at the office first. I'm sure Eloise won't mind my taking the morning off, but I have a report on my desk that I need to complete final edits on, then print and deliver to her."

"In that case, why don't you come to the courtroom when you're finished with the report. You can sit in on the morning session, and I'll take you to lunch afterward."

"That sounds lovely." Allison glanced at her

watch. ''I'd better hurry or I'll be late.'' She slipped out of her chair and carried her plate and cup to the sink to rinse before tucking them into the dishwasher.

Jorge rose and held her jacket for her, his hands lingering on her upper arms when she looked over her shoulder at him. He couldn't resist dropping a quick hard kiss on her mouth and was rewarded with a quick flush of color in her cheeks, her amber eyes going faintly smoky.

He knew that look. His hands tightened for a moment but then he released her and stepped back.

''We'll be late if we don't hurry.'' His voice was lower, husky with the desire that pumped through his veins.

''Yes. Of course.'' Her lashes lowered, shielding her eyes from him, and she walked quickly to the entryway to collect her coat.

He swallowed a sigh and cleared his own dishes, rinsing and putting them in the dishwasher with quick efficiency before following her. They shared a taxi, Allison exiting first in front of her building.

''I'll see you later this morning,'' he said, after getting out to hold the door for her.

She nodded, smiling with anticipation, and he reentered the cab, turning to watch her slim figure disappear into the building as the taxi moved on.

Allison was late. Editing the report for Eloise had taken longer than she'd anticipated, and it was after ten-thirty and the morning recess before she slipped into the courtroom and found an empty slot near the back. The seats in the wood-paneled room were nearly filled with observers, including a number of reporters, family members, attorneys and individuals interested in the high-profile trial. The jury box was empty, the group excused while the defense and prosecution presented arguments regarding a point of law governing admission of exhibits submitted by the prosecution.

Allison slipped off her coat, the room being warm from the presence of so many people, and settled in to listen. She didn't recognize the attorney speaking, but it quickly became clear that he was a member of the defense team.

Like everyone else in the audience, she listened closely while the attorney argued passionately about the prejudicial impact of the photographs on the jury.

Photographs? Allison peered around the bulk of the large man sitting in front of her and located the three large displays held by easels, angled to one side of the judge's bench where both the court and audience could view them clearly. She dragged in a swift breath. Pinned to the white boards were a series of twelve-by-fifteen photographs. Graphic and brutal, they depicted the crime scene. There was no question that they were shocking.

Also there was no question why the prosecution wanted them to go before the jury, she thought. They were vivid proof that a horrific, violent crime had taken place.

The attorney completed his argument and took his seat at counsel table.

The judge, a distinguished gentleman in black robes with a touch of silver at his temples, peered over his glasses. "Mr. Perez, rebuttal?"

"Yes, Your Honor."

Jorge stood and walked to the easels with their stark photos. Allison listened, totally absorbed as he made an impressively logical case for the inclusion of the exhibits in their entirety.

When he finished, the judge asked several questions regarding case law supporting both prosecution and defense positions on their arguments. While both attorneys' responses were well thought out, Allison was impressed by Jorge's. Hearing him quote case law with split-second, incisive clarity not only made her respect for his ability as an attorney grow by leaps and bounds, it also made her apprehensive. He was clearly brilliant, his razor-sharp mind and commanding presence giving him the same above-the-crowd prominence in the courtroom that her father held in the film world.

Allison's heart twisted with apprehension. That kind of brilliance and competency in his career could blind him to anything beyond his work, if he let it. Just as her father's single-minded focus on his career had blinded him to her needs as a child, so might Jorge be unable to see how much their baby needed him.

And me. She thought, the realization painful. *Will he be able to see how much I need him? And if he does, will he care?*

While she was lost in thought, the judge advised counsel that he would render his decision on the exhibits after lunch. Meanwhile, he ordered the bailiff to remove the easels and the exhibits in question and to return the jury to the courtroom.

When the jury members were reseated, the judge re-called the witness, Henry Jackson, to the stand.

Allison twisted in her seat and watched the heavyset, middle-aged accountant enter the courtroom and walk to the witness stand.

''I will remind you, Mr. Jackson, that you are still under oath.'' The judge waited until Mr. Jackson nodded his understanding before he waved a hand at Jorge. ''Your witness, Mr. Perez.''

''Thank you, Your Honor.'' Jorge stood, consulted his notes for a moment and approached the witness stand.

Allison knew that Henry Jackson was a pivotal witness in Jorge's case, being the accountant for the defendant and his deceased business partner. Jorge had told her that motivation for the murder was a disagreement between the two men over the profits from construction of a multistorey hotel in New Jersey. The accountant was reluctant to testify because his bookkeeping practices teetered on the edge of illegal.

She leaned forward, fascinated, as Jorge began his examination with a deceptively mild approach, drawing the witness into a small admission of duplicity. Having gained that crack in the witness's story, Jorge swiftly annihilated the man's position with an incisive, aggressive examination that was ruthless. Brilliant, Allison conceded, but unquestionably ruthless.

He was intimidating. Shaken by this insight into her new husband, Allison couldn't help but question her ability to handle him. He'd psychologically overpowered the witness, and Henry Jackson's helplessness somehow reminded her of the night when she'd been physically overpowered by the egotistical young movie actor and had been unable to prevent his forcing her.

Had she made a fatal error and married the wrong person? Would she be able to hold her own with a man whose personality was as powerful as Jorge's?

Disturbed by the direction of her thoughts, Allison wrote a brief note canceling their luncheon date, using an urgent meeting at Manhattan Multiples as an excuse. Then she quietly rose and made her way to the back of the courtroom, pausing at the door to ask a bailiff to deliver her note to Jorge.

Too upset to face returning to the office immediately, she stopped in at the coffee bar. Zoe looked up when the door opened and flashed a welcoming smile before handing a customer his change.

Allison stood in line, waiting patiently until the two men ahead of her had been served. At last it was her turn.

"Hi, Allison. What are you doing away from the office this early?" Zoe's curves were enveloped in a bibbed white apron with "barista" appliquéd in scarlet on the top left corner below her name. Her uniform of black slacks and long-sleeved white shirt was further brightened by the red scrunchy that held her black hair in a ponytail, and matching red hoop earrings.

"I've been at the courthouse." Allison ran her fingers through her hair, pushing it behind her ear in a nervous gesture.

"Oh?" Zoe frowned at Allison's telltale gesture. "It's time for my break. Want to share a chai tea with me?"

"I'd love to." Allison nodded, before remembering to add, "Decaf for me, please."

"Sure. Why don't you grab a table—maybe the one in the back corner that just emptied. I'll be right with you and bring our drinks."

"Great." Allison shrugged out of her coat as she walked to the rear of the cozy coffee shop with its collection of small tables, a couple of worn Victorian plush sofas and three comfortable armchairs tucked into angles and corners, and a scattering of daily newspapers strewn about on seats and table-tops. She hung her coat over the back of a wooden chair, tucked her purse beneath the seat and was just sitting down when Zoe arrived with their tea.

"Here you go." Zoe set the hot mugs on the little round café table and plopped into the chair opposite, eyeing Allison with concern. "Pardon me for saying so, hon, but you look like you've just lost your last friend." She grinned. "And I know that's not true, 'cause you've still got me."

A reluctant smile curved Allison's lips. "And that's a blessing, Zoe." Already cheered by Zoe's warm, blunt honesty, Allison felt her tense muscles ease. She rubbed her forehead.

"So, tell me. What happened? 'Cause if the gorgeous Assistant D.A. isn't treating you right, I'll give the twins a call." Zoe sipped her tea, clearly expecting Allison to share whatever was causing the worry lines on her brow.

And that, Allison reflected, is exactly why I came here.

A warm rush of affection further eased her tension, and she smiled ruefully. "Have I ever told you how much I appreciate you for being my friend?"

"Yes, but feel free to tell me as often as you like." Zoe's grin flashed once again before she sobered. "What's wrong, Allison?"

"I sat in on the murder trial this morning—the one that Jorge's prosecuting."

"And...?" Zoe prompted when Allison fell silent for a long moment.

"And watching him question a hostile defense witness was a little scary."

"Scary?" Zoe frowned. "How do you mean, scary?"

"Scary, as in—he was absolutely ruthless, Zoe. The witness didn't stand a chance."

"You mean Jorge did something unethical?"

"Oh, no." Allison shook her head. "Not at all, his cross-exam was brilliant. He's an amazing attorney."

"So he did something right?" Zoe was clearly confused.

"Yes, his legal work was terrific. What bothered me was that he was ruthless. Seeing him in action in the courtroom was alarming. And if he's like that in the courtroom, what if he's capable of that same level of ruthlessness in his personal life? I'm having serious doubts as to whether I could cope with him."

Zoe's face cleared, her gaze softening. "Oh, Allison, there's a huge difference between a man's approach to his work and his dealings with the people he loves. And there's no question that he's crazy about you."

Startled, Allison stared at Zoe. "What makes you think that?"

"Because I watched the two of you during your wedding. He couldn't take his eyes off you. The guy is head-over-heels, completely zonked, crazy about you. Trust me, I know when a guy's hooked. And Jorge is."

Allison was unconvinced, but Zoe was adamant. They finished their tea and Zoe returned to pouring coffee after getting a promise from Allison that they would get together for lunch the following week.

Slightly reassured by Zoe's comments, but still not sure of Jorge, Allison returned to the office and tried to focus on work. But she achieved little, for she couldn't put the image of Jorge's powerful presence in court out of her mind. As an attorney she admired his work, but as a woman she felt threatened by the possibility that he might apply that same ruthlessness to his personal life.

Late that afternoon someone rapped on her door.

"Yes?" Allison called.

The door opened partway and Josie poked her head in. "Eloise wants us all in the main conference room for a meeting in ten minutes."

"Okay. Do you know what it's about?" Allison asked.

"Nope. She just buzzed me and asked me to round up everybody in the office. She stressed 'ev-

erybody' so I'm guessing that she has an announcement of some sort."

"Okay, I'm on my way."

Josie whisked away, and Allison closed the open
file on her desk and made her way to the conference
room. Eloise stood at the far end of the long table.
Allison took a seat halfway down, next to the
heavily pregnant Leah. The chairs quickly filled
with the rest of the staff. Josie came in last and
dropped into the empty seat next to Allison.

Eloise glanced up and down the table, silently
counting bodies, and with a decisive nod, rapped
on the walnut tabletop to gather everyone's attention.

"I asked you all here to share some unfortunate
news with you."

The staff exchanged worried glances. Eloise's
normally upbeat personality was muted, and her obvious concern was felt by everyone in the room.
Allison felt a chilling sense of foreboding.

"I've exhausted the last of my hopes for alter-
native funding," Eloise continued, her voice heavy
with defeat. "And I thought it best that I tell you
sooner rather than later. It seems inevitable that
when our current funding from the city expires,
Manhattan Multiples will have to close its doors."

Lara Mancini, seated across the table from Allison, gasped, her green eyes round with shock.

For Allison, already feeling frazzled and upset by

her morning spent watching Jorge in court, Eloise's announcement was one unexpected blow too many. Her usual calm control disintegrated.

"But you can't close our doors. I'm pregnant!" And to her horror, she burst into tears.

Startled, her co-workers were shocked into silence for one brief second.

"You're our mysterious pregnant person?" Eloise's stunned comment was echoed around the table.

"No way!" Josie burst out, then winced and wrapped an arm around Allison's quivering shoulders. "Sorry, Allison, it's just that you're the last person I'd ever guessed to be our mystery woman. You spend all your time working and studying, who'd have thought it was you?"

"So that's why you were married so quickly!" Leah exclaimed, then clapped a hand to her mouth.

Allison wanted to respond, but she was incapable of speech. Instead she cried harder.

"Come with me, dear." Eloise rounded the table and gently urged the still-sobbing Allison out of her chair. Wrapping an arm around her, she guided her away from the sympathetic but amazed fellow employees and into the privacy of her office.

Chapter Eight

"Sit here, I'll find a box of tissues." Eloise gently urged Allison to a seat on the sofa in her office and left her for a moment.

Allison was appalled at her outburst, but she couldn't seem to stop crying, although the sobs had diminished to a trickle of tears. She looked up when Eloise returned with a box of tissues and a glass of water.

"I'm sorry, Eloise—I don't know what's wrong with me lately," she managed to say, pulling a handful of tissues out of the box and dabbing at her eyes and damp cheeks. "I just can't seem to stop crying. I feel like a leaky faucet."

Eloise smiled and held out a glass of water. "Don't worry, Allison, it's perfectly normal for a pregnant woman to feel weepy. Lots of women go through this, and hopefully your emotions will calm down in the second trimester."

"Really?" Allison fervently hoped Eloise was right about this. Normally calm and collected, she was mortified by her emotional outburst in the meeting.

"Yes. I have a very good pregnancy information book with a section on the emotional impact of pregnancy. I'll be glad to lend it to you, if you'd like."

"I bought four books on pregnancy and child-birth," Allison confessed. "But I've been so busy with exams that I've only read a few chapters." She buried her face in her hands. "I'm going to be a terrible mother, Eloise. I haven't even read all the books yet."

"Nonsense." Eloise patted her shoulder. "You'll be a wonderful mother. And you have months still to find time to read the books." She shook her head. "I must say, Allison, I'm amazed that you're my mysterious pregnant employee. Why didn't you tell me? Was there a reason you felt compelled to keep this a secret?"

Allison lifted her head. "I'm terrified, Eloise."

"Terrified? Why, for heaven's sake?"

"Because everything happened so fast." She

waved a hand, and dabbed at the tears that kept overflowing and trickling down her cheeks. "It was such a shock when I discovered that I was pregnant. And then Jorge found me, and I accidentally told him that I was pregnant, and he insisted we get married, and then we *did* get married, and—" she paused to draw breath "—and I feel as if I've been caught up in a whirlwind. Not to mention…" She paused, her worried gaze searching Eloise's sympathetic face.

"Yes?" Eloise prompted.

"I'm terrified that something's wrong," she whispered. "I'm only two months along and my body is changing so quickly. Yesterday I noticed that my tummy is already visibly growing and my skirts are too tight at the waist. I can't button them or my slacks." She pressed a hand to her stomach where her skirt, always discreetly loose, was now snug, the caramel wool stretched across the outward curve.

Eloise lifted a brow as she followed the movement of Allison's hand, her eyes widening. Then a delighted smile formed on her lips, and she beamed at Allison. "I don't think there's anything wrong, Allison. I think you're carrying more than one baby."

"No." Allison shook her head vehemently. "No, that's not possible. I can't imagine having one

baby, let alone two.'' Her eyes widened in panic.
''Or more.''

''Trust me,'' Eloise said comfortingly, patting
her hand once more. ''You'll adjust. Two or three
babies aren't that much more difficult than one, especially since Jorge can afford to have a nanny in
to help you. And they're two and three times the
joy as they grow, so it's a blessing, really.''

Eloise had the experience to know, given that she
was the mother of triplet sons, but Allison still
wasn't convinced that she herself would handle
multiple babies as well. Goodness, she wasn't sure
that she could handle a single baby with any degree
of competency.

The mere thought of giving birth to more than
one child had her hyperventilating.

''How long before I'll know for sure if I'm carrying more than one baby?'' she asked.

''Call your doctor and ask her,'' Eloise advised.
''I don't remember how far along I was before I
found out, but your doctor can tell you if having an
ultrasound can tell you immediately.''

''I'll go call her now.'' Allison stood, clutching
a handful of soggy tissues, her expression both determined and worried.

Eloise rose with her, smiling warmly. ''I think
that's an excellent idea, Allison. And try not to
worry,'' she added. ''Whether it's one baby, or
more, you're going to be a terrific mother.''

"How do you know?" Allison asked, unconvinced.

"Because I know you," Eloise spoke with conviction. "Now go call your doctor. The sooner you know, the sooner you'll relax."

Allison doubted that she'd relax, regardless of the outcome of the ultrasound, but she murmured her thanks and left Eloise's office for her own. Fortunately for her peace of mind, her doctor was able to fit in an appointment for her the following afternoon.

Jorge knew that Allison was worried about something. Despite her repeated, rather distracted, assurances that she was "fine," he didn't believe her.

Standing at the sink, rinsing dishes after dinner, he glanced sideways at her. She stood beside him, taking the rinsed plates, glasses, silverware and miscellaneous chinaware from him and slotting them into the dishwasher.

Normally this part of the evening was relaxed and easy, since they'd both had time to unwind after a long day at the office, had filled hungry stomachs and were looking forward to a quiet evening. Tonight, however, he could see the tension in her shoulders and the tiny frown lines between her brows.

"That's the last dirty dish," he announced, turning off the water and drying his hands. "What do you want to do tonight? Watch TV or a movie maybe?''

''No, I don't think so.'' Allison gave him a small smile, dropped a tablet of soap into the dishwasher's compartment and closed the door. She frowned at the settings, then pushed the appropriate buttons.

''How about poker?'' Jorge crossed his arms over his chest, leaned his hip against the counter and eyed her. ''I'll let you cheat all you want,'' he teased.

''Thanks, but I don't feel like playing cards tonight.''

She drifted toward the living room, and Jorge followed, watching her settle on to the sofa, pull a fat velvet pillow onto her lap and stare unseeingly at the blank television screen.

Frustrated at her unwillingness to talk to him, he shored up his patience and followed her, dropping on to the sofa to face her.

''Hey,'' he said gently, waiting until she looked at him before he continued. ''Are you going to tell me what's bothering you?''

She gave him yet another of those worried, faintly fearful glances that he'd been receiving all evening. Her fingers nervously twisted the fringe edging the soft pillow, twining it through her fingers.

What the hell is going on? Tamping down his

inclination to demand an explanation, he covered her fingers with his, gently stilling their movements. When he stroked the smooth skin on the back of her hand with his forefinger, she trembled, gradually easing as he threaded her fingers through his. He lifted her hand and trapped her palm against his cheek, his gaze searching hers.

"What's wrong, sweetheart? You've been worried about something all night, I can tell." He smoothed his free hand over the silky fall of her hair from crown to cheek, then tucked the satiny strands behind her ear.

Her eyes softened, the tension easing from her slim frame. "I am a bit concerned about something Eloise told me today. I didn't want to tell you until I know for certain if we have anything to worry about."

"Tell me now," he murmured. "I hate to know you're fretting about something all alone. Isn't that what marriage is about? Sharing?"

She gave him a small smile and nodded. "Yes, you're right of course. I'm not used to having someone to talk to when I'm worried."

He smoothed a forefinger between her brows, easing away the little frown lines. "Well now you have someone. So tell me, what did Eloise tell you that has you so concerned?"

Allison bit her lip uncertainly, a small silence falling between them. Jorge waited patiently.

"A couple of things, actually," she said at last.

Jorge was silent, hoping his patience would encourage her to confide in him, and was rewarded when she drew a deep breath and continued.

"She called a staff meeting this afternoon to announce that there's a very real possibility that Manhattan Multiples will have to close its doors when the current funding expires."

The little frown lines appeared again between her brows. Jorge restrained the urge to smooth them away once more.

"So I may be unemployed in a few months. And I don't know how I'll pay for law school tuition without an income."

Jorge gave up the battle and leaned forward, gently kissing the spot between her brows where the tiny lines puckered her smooth skin. He felt them ease away under his lips. He lifted his head to look at her.

"Honey, I can afford your tuition." Her gaze searched his and he spoke quickly, forestalling the protest he felt sure she was about to voice. "And if you won't accept it as an outright gift from your husband, then we can call it a loan, and when you're a very rich, very successful, very famous attorney, you can pay me back, okay?"

She stared at him, undecided for a long moment. Jorge knew the moment he won, for her mouth quirked into a small smile just before her nod confirmed his reading of her expression.

"Okay." The word was soft, husky with appreciation.

"What else did Eloise say today that you're worried about?"

Swift apprehension darkened her amber eyes, and Jorge almost groaned at the quick return of worry to her delicate features.

"Well—" she hesitated, her lashes lowering, concealing her thoughts from him "—I don't know if you've noticed, but I've gained several pounds in the past two weeks."

Jorge managed not to give in to the delighted grin that threatened. He glanced down at her midriff, where one slender hand lay over the shirt that he knew covered jeans with the top button undone. "No," he lied. "I hadn't. You look perfect to me."

The glance she shot him was skeptical. "You haven't noticed that the baby is growing and that my tummy is bigger than it was last week?"

Carefully he moved her hand from his cheek and laid it against his thigh. Then he leaned closer and placed his palms on her midriff, just below her breasts, and smoothed them out and downward, past her waist, then inward until they lay over hers and the growing small bulge beneath.

"Hmm," he commented, his voice slightly rougher, his pulse throbbing harder at the feel of her beneath his hands. "You're going to need some new jeans soon." He glanced up to find her cheeks faintly flushed with color and knew a fierce satisfaction that placing his hands on her affected her as strongly as it did him.

"Yes," she murmured. "Eloise thinks I might be carrying more than one baby."

He stared at her, astounded. "Twins? Are you sure?"

"I don't know." Her voice was anxious. "But I'm growing faster than I think I should be at this stage. I know from talking to expectant mothers at Manhattan Multiples that twins or triplets tend to run in families. Are there twins in your family?"

Jorge paused to think, a small smile breaking over his face. "Yes, there are. In fact, there are two sets of twins on my father's side of the family."

"Oh, my goodness." Distressed, Allison pushed at his hands. "Why didn't you tell me?"

"I didn't think of it," he said reasonably. "Besides, there isn't anything we can do about it at this point, is there?"

"No, but you could have warned me. I would have been more prepared. I'm not sure I can be a good mother to one baby, let alone two. And what if there are more than two?"

The sheer panic on her face sobered Jorge. Without pausing to think about it, he wrapped his arms around her and pulled her onto his lap, tucking her head against his shoulder.

"Sweetheart," he murmured, concerned. "You're going to be the world's best mom, no matter how many babies we have."

"How can you know that?" she nearly wailed.

"Because—" he tilted her face up to his "—you care. And you want this baby, just as badly as I do."

"You'll help me, right?"

"Absolutely."

The panic in her amber eyes subsided, but worry still lurked there. Baffled, Jorge searched her face, his thumb smoothing over the soft skin of her cheek. "Honey, is there something else bothering you? Something about the baby that you haven't told me?"

"Can we keep her safe?" Allison whispered. "I don't want anyone to hurt her."

Her fingers gripped his T-shirt, the soft cotton bunching in her tight grip.

"I'll guard her with my life, Allison, I swear," he said solemnly, a sense of foreboding filling him as he watched the fear in her eyes. "Who hurt you, Allison?" Her gaze flickered away from his and she buried her face against his chest, the soft silk of her hair brushing the underside of his chin. "Tell me, sweetheart." Silence followed and he added softly,

"Hey, we share, remember? You're not alone anymore."

Slowly, her voice at times so soft that he could barely hear her, Allison told him about her lonely childhood. When she reached her teenage years and in halting words related the details of the night she was forced by a career-conscious young actor prominent in her parents' world, Jorge swore, his arms tightening protectively as her tears soaked his shirt.

"No wonder you're worried about our baby," he growled, furious that the vulnerable girl she'd been at seventeen had been treated with so little care and protection. His hand closed gently over her hair, and he tugged her face up to his. "I swear to you, Allison, I'll never let anyone harm you or our baby. Never."

The fierce words slowly erased the last remnants of fear and worry lurking in her eyes. Jorge gave a deep sigh of relief when she released his shirt, circled his neck with her arms and let her eyes drift closed as her mouth sought his.

Allison felt so cherished by Jorge's response to her worries that she floated on air the next day. Although neither of them had said "I love you," she felt immeasurably reassured that their marriage and life together had a chance of being happy. When he learned that she'd scheduled an ultrasound with her doctor the following afternoon, Jorge had insisted on being present.

Dr. Kenyan's office was closer to Jorge's office than hers, so Allison left early and caught a taxi, intending to surprise him. She paused at the reception desk, waiting patiently as the receptionist dealt with a difficult phone call while other lines rang incessantly. At last the young woman disconnected the call, quickly put several others on hold and looked at Allison. "Sorry to keep you waiting. Whom are you here to see?"

"Jorge Perez."

"Right." The harried young woman answered a ringing telephone, listened for a moment, then held her palm over the receiver. "I think he's in his office—you can go on back." She gestured toward a door to the left of her desk. "Through that door, down the hall, fifth door on the right."

"Thank you." The heavy oak door to the left of the reception area opened on to a long hall lined with offices. The doors to three of them stood open, and Allison glanced into them as she walked past. One was empty, two had men in shirtsleeves and ties talking on the phone, seated behind large desks. All of them had overflowing in-boxes and stacks of files and law books piled on every available flat surface.

Two women in dark suits, briefcases in hand, moved quickly past Allison and through the door behind her, giving her distracted nods as they hurried off. Somewhere down the hall, phones were ringing and a burst of laughter made Allison suspect that the secretarial support staff probably had their offices there.

The fifth office door on the right was closed. Allison smiled with anticipation and with a quick rap of knuckles on the thick oak panel, turned the knob and pushed the door inward.

She gasped, her hand frozen on the doorknob, unable to move, unable to breathe. Jorge stood across the room, the early afternoon sunshine pouring through the window to frame his body, his arms wrapped around a slim blond woman. Her face was buried against his chest, and she glanced over his shoulder, her blue eyes misty, at the same time that Jorge looked up and saw Allison.

He looked stunned. For a long moment Allison felt frozen, as if the three of them were a trio of statues. Then pain shafted through the shock, making her shudder from the impact, nearly sending her to her knees. Her first instinct was to run, and she obeyed it without question. Curiously detached, she moved swiftly down the hall, vaguely aware that Jorge called her name. Then she was out of the office, in the main hallway, where an elevator was just beginning to close its doors.

"Wait!" She ran across the marble floor and slipped inside. As the doors eased shut, she caught a quick glimpse of Jorge, just opening the hall door of the D.A.'s office, his face dark with anger.

She shivered, the cold chill reaching through the numbness and ice that encased her emotions.

No. She pushed the pain away, refused to feel. Not now. Not until she was alone, someplace where strangers wouldn't watch her fall apart.

But the shiver had cracked the ice that protected her, and Allison could feel the shield breaking up. She knew that the cold numbness was the only thing keeping her from falling apart. She looked frantically at the floor indicator and realized that she was several floors up from the main lobby and escape from the building.

The elevator eased to a stop, the doors slid open. Allison joined the exodus on to the third floor, searching frantically until she located a sign listing the offices on this level and the location of the women's rest room. She moved down the hall as swiftly as possible on legs that felt distinctly unsteady, turning the corner and quickly entering the sanctuary of the ladies' room.

A solitary occupant, washing her hands at one of the porcelain sinks, looked up. Allison couldn't manage to answer the woman's polite smile, needing all her concentration to reach the safety of a stall. Her fingers fumbled the latch closed, and she leaned her forehead against the metal panel, body tense, eyes closed as she drew in deep breaths in an attempt to control her sobs.

The outer door opened, then closed with an audible thud as the other woman left the room. Allison sagged against the door, giving in to the tearing sobs that shook her body while tears poured down her face.

Dear God, it hurts. She hugged her arms around her midriff, the ache physical and much too agonizing. *Who was the woman?*

Too late to worry about whether she might fall in love with Jorge. Much too late, she realized. She'd already fallen.

And he didn't love her. The tender expression on his face as he'd looked down at the woman in his arms had been all too revealing.

The knowledge sent fresh pain slicing through her heart.

Allison lost track of time. The tearing sobs that shook her slowly subsided and she wiped her eyes, blew her nose and glanced at her watch, relieved to see that she still had plenty of time before her doctor's appointment. She left the stall, wincing when she saw her red-rimmed, swollen eyes reflected in the mirror above the row of white sinks. She folded paper towels and ran cold water over them, applying the cool, wet towels to her eyes and flushed cheeks until the swelling subsided and the red eased to pink. Then she carefully applied makeup, and at last, satisfied that the casual observer wouldn't find anything startling in her appearance, left the ladies' room. She'd been in the bathroom for more than forty minutes, and though she doubted that Jorge would still be searching for her, she was nonetheless relieved when she exited the building and caught a cab without seeing him.

Despite her shattered emotions, she was determined to get through the day without falling apart again. And she was just as determined not to let Jorge know how badly she'd been hurt by seeing him with another woman.

He only married me because of the baby, not because he cares about me. She repeated the words over and over, hoping that the reminder would force her to accept the unwanted truth. Until she opened the door and saw him with his arms around the pretty blonde, she hadn't realized how much she'd been hoping and dreaming that he would come to feel more than responsibility toward her.

She managed to smile pleasantly at the nurse in the reception area and make appropriate replies as she was weighed and her blood pressure checked. Then the nurse left her while she changed into a blue paper gown. Allison clutched the gown around her and climbed onto the exam table, tucking the white sheet up to her waist. Brooding, she stared at her bare feet dangling above the floor, toenails painted hot pink, and wondered how long she would have to wait before the doctor arrived.

The door opened and she looked up, forcing a small smile.

But it wasn't Dr. Kenyan that entered. It was Jorge.

Her smile disappeared. "What are you doing here?"

"You're having an ultrasound. I told you last night that I'd be here."

"I wish you'd leave."

His eyes were turbulent, the hard bones of his face clenched. "I knew you jumped to the wrong conclusions. That wasn't what you thought it was, Allison."

"What wasn't what I thought it was?" She refused to make this easy for him; she wanted him gone. She was terrified that she was either going to throw something at him or burst into tears. Either option was appalling.

"What you saw when you walked into my office." He shoved his hands into the pockets of his suit slacks, his big frame tense. "The woman you saw was Mrs. MacAfee and she's the widow of the victim in a murder case I'm handling. I'd just told her that the man who murdered her husband confessed and would be going to prison."

"I see." Allison looked away from him, staring

at her fingers where they gripped the edge of the white, hospital-issue cotton sheet.

"No," he ground out. "I don't think you do. She broke down and cried when I told her, and I was comforting her. That's all, Allison. There was absolutely nothing sexual about what you saw."

Allison was torn. She badly wanted to believe him, but the sight of him holding another woman in his arms had shattered her fragile trust in him and her belief in her own role as a woman he desired.

"Allison, I have no interest in other women. I don't want you to stay with me just to make a home for our baby. I want us to have a real marriage."

She stared at him helplessly, wanting desperately to tell him that she loved him and wanted him to truly be her husband, but unable to voice the yearning that filled her. He hadn't said that he loved her, and her bruised heart badly needed to hear the words. "I...I don't know—"

A brisk rap on the door interrupted her, the sharp sound quickly followed by the doctor's entrance.

"Good afternoon, Allison." Dr. Kenyan's keen gaze swept her and Jorge, shrewdly assessing their tense figures. "And who is this?"

"I'm the father—and Allison's husband." Jorge managed a tight smile for the friendly doctor and held out his hand. "Jorge Perez, Dr. Kenyan."

"Ah. Delighted to meet you." Dr. Kenyan shook

Jorge's hand, and she smiled at Allison. "I understand that we're going to do an ultrasound to determine if you might be carrying twins, is that right?"

"Yes." Allison didn't look at Jorge, focusing instead on the doctor's kind face. "I've just recently learned that Jorge has twins on his father's side of the family."

"I see." Dr. Kenyan flashed a grin that lit her pleasant features. "So, there's a history of multiple births in your family, Mr. Perez?"

"Yes," Jorge confirmed. "Two sets of twins, actually."

"Well, that might increase your chances." The doctor tucked her pen in the pocket of her lab coat and slid Allison's file on to the counter. She snapped off the overhead light before perching on the high stool beside the exam table. "I've discussed the procedure with Allison, Mr. Perez, but so you'll understand what we're going to do, let me explain."

Jorge listened intently as Dr. Kenyan explained the painless procedure, nodding at intervals.

"Do you have any questions?" the doctor asked, finally.

"No, it seems fairly straightforward."

"Good." She nodded emphatically. "You might want to step a bit closer so you can have a clear view of the screen and see what Allison and I see."

Jorge complied, and Allison stiffened as his coat sleeve brushed her bare arm.

Dr. Kenyan finished turning knobs and adjusting dials, and with efficient movements, bared Allison's midsection, the sheet and gown modestly covering all but her tummy.

"The gel is going to feel a little cool, Allison," the doctor warned, just before she placed the slippery wand on Allison's stomach.

"Oh!" Allison flinched at the odd sensation. It felt as if the doctor were smoothing Jell-O over her skin.

"All right?" Dr. Kenyan scanned Allison's face.

"Yes. It just feels strange."

Dr. Kenyan smiled. "I know. Now just lie still and we'll see what we can find."

She continued to move the wand over Allison's tummy, watching the screen and adjusting knobs as she did so.

Allison and Jorge stared at the screen the doctor focused on, but neither could make out anything that looked like a baby.

"Aha," the doctor murmured with satisfaction.

"What?" Jorge and Allison spoke in unison.

"You were right. There are two babies."

Jorge's hand closed over Allison's where it lay atop the sheet, and she instinctively turned her palm up to his, her fingers gripping him tightly.

"You're sure?" she asked, staring at the screen

and its black-and-white smears and waves. "I can't see babies."

"Let me see if I can get a clearer view for you." Dr. Kenyan moved the wand.

Allison and Jorge collectively held their breath.

"There we are." The doctor's voice held satisfaction. She traced the forefinger of her free hand over the screen as she spoke. "You see these two very dark oblong sections outlined in white? Inside each of these is this tiny lighter area, shaped rather like an upside-down Kewpie doll—those are your two babies." She turned, smiling widely. "Congratulations, Mommy and Daddy, you're having twins."

Allison jerked upright on the table. Her gaze flew to meet Jorge's and saw awe, shock, delight, all mixed with the same faint panic that she felt.

"Twins," he repeated, his voice rough with emotion. He shook his head and looked at the doctor. "You're sure? There couldn't be any mistake?"

"No mistake. There are definitely two babies."

"Oh, my goodness." Allison's voice was faint. She didn't realize that she still gripped Jorge's fingers tightly until he lifted her hand and pressed a kiss against her knuckles. She could only stare at him, torn between the panic and joy that filled her at the thought of having two babies instead of one, and the unresolved argument that lay between them.

"If you'll have a seat in the reception area, Mr.

Perez, I'm going to do a pelvic exam of Allison, and then we can meet in my office, where I'll be happy to answer any further questions you might have.''

Jorge shot back his cuff and frowned at his watch. ''Will it take long, Doctor? I have a meeting with a judge and defense counsel in a half hour and they can't proceed without me.''

''We'll probably be fifteen or twenty minutes.''

Jorge looked at Allison. ''Then I'm afraid I can't stay. Can we have an appointment later this week to discuss the twins?''

''Of course.''

''Thank you, Dr. Kenyan.'' His fingers tightened over Allison's. ''I'll see you tonight.''

The words were a promise as well as a question, and Allison could only nod.

Jorge searched her pale features, his gaze intense, before he reluctantly released her, nodded to the doctor and abruptly left the room.

Allison sighed, frowning at the closed door. Had he meant what he said earlier about wanting a real marriage? How did he really feel about having two babies instead of one?

''I have the distinct impression that the two of you aren't in accord about your pregnancy. Does he have reservations about the two of you becoming parents?''

Dr. Kenyan's blunt statement caught Allison's attention, yanking her back to the present with a vengeance.

"Oh, no, Jorge is looking forward to being a father. He's been wonderfully supportive." Allison shoved her fingers through her hair and pushed it away from her face. "I'm the one that's having second thoughts."

"You're considering terminating the pregnancy?"

The calm question shocked Allison. "No! Oh, no. Absolutely not."

The doctor smiled at her vehement, instant response and settled more comfortably onto her stool, eyeing Allison. "Then suppose you tell me what's worrying you."

"I'm not sure I'll be a good mother," she said cautiously.

"And why is that?" The good doctor didn't appear shocked. In fact, her kind face reflected only interest and good humor.

"Well, for one thing," Allison said slowly, "ever since I took the pregnancy test, I've noticed that I'm crying over the smallest of things. And I'm having mood swings—one minute I'm perfectly happy and the next I'm horribly blue. And for no good reason." She frowned unhappily at the doctor. "I don't know how Jorge can bear to live with me, Doctor. It's awful."

"Are these normal occurrences for you, Allison?

Did you have mood swings before you became pregnant?"

"No. I've never been like this."

Dr. Kenyan laughed and patted Allison's clasped hands where they gripped the white sheet. "Then I feel safe in saying that what you're experiencing is quite probably a case of your hormones struggling to adjust to the pregnancy."

"Then I won't be like this forever?"

"No."

Allison heaved a sigh of relief. Although she'd often heard the nurses and other staff at Manhattan Multiples talk about the emotional highs and lows that could afflict a woman during pregnancy, she'd been convinced that what she was feeling was radically out of the normal range. "Thank goodness. I thought I might be suffering some sort of emotional breakdown."

Dr. Kenyan queried her further and after several moments, smiled gently. "I think what you're feeling is heightened by the stress of being a newlywed. The less stress you have, the better it is for you and for the baby. Are you and your husband having any problems? Because if you are," she added when Allison hesitated, "perhaps you might consider that with your hormones struggling to adjust to the baby, your perspective is likely to be slightly skewed."

After speaking with the doctor for a full half hour

instead of the fifteen minutes she'd predicted that the exam would take, Allison had much to think about.

Still mulling over Dr. Kenyan's words, Allison returned to the office to find the staff in an uproar. Josie shrieked with delight when Allison walked through the door, but Allison couldn't understand her.

"What is it? What's happened?"

"Leah had her babies!" Josie's smile beamed, her eyes misty with emotion.

Chapter Nine

"When?" Allison was shocked. "I've only been gone from the office for a few hours!"

"I know. Isn't it exciting?"

"Yes, very exciting." Allison realized belatedly that Josie was wearing her coat. Lara Mancini hurried down the hall and joined them, her green eyes sparkling with delight.

"Allison, did you hear?"

"I just told her," Josie put in.

Tony Martino pushed open the outer door and peered in, a warm jacket covering his broad shoulders. "Anybody want to share a taxi?"

"Absolutely." Lara slung her purse over her arm and walked quickly toward him.

''Where are we going?'' Allison asked, feeling a step out of sync with the others.

''To the hospital.'' Josie pulled on her gloves and grabbed her purse from the top of her desk. ''Eloise left as soon as she heard that Leah had delivered the babies, and she told the rest of us that we could lock up and join her, unless we had appointments that couldn't be canceled.'' She glanced down the hall at the dark offices. ''And I think just about everybody else raced out of here. We may be the last to leave.''

''I can't wait to see the babies,'' Lara commented, as Allison and Josie joined her and Tony in the hall. Josie locked the doors behind them, and they hurried toward the elevators.

''Did Leah have any problems giving birth?'' Allison asked.

''No, Eloise said the doctors were pleased with everything.''

''Excellent.'' Allison had worried about how well Leah would do during delivery, since it seemed the soon-to-be mother had grown bigger each day.

''I don't know how you women do it,'' Tony commented, shaking his head. ''One baby is a lot of work, but three seems darned near impossible.''

''Eloise assures me that two or three babies aren't all that much more difficult than one,'' Allison commented without thinking.

"Yeah?" Tony eyed her with friendly curiosity.

"Yes," she kept her voice casual. She didn't want to give away her new status as a multiple-birth mom. Not yet. "She has triplets."

The others took their cue from her noncommittal reply, and the four chatted about a variety of topics as they rode to the hospital and found the proper floor.

The waiting room was filled with their co-workers from Manhattan Multiples, and they were greeted with a chorus of hellos.

"How's Leah?" Allison asked. "And the babies?"

"She's doing very well," Eloise said, her smile bright. "And the babies are just wonderful—three perfect little girls. Leah named them Allison, Josie and Eloise. Isn't that the sweetest thing?"

"Oh, yes." Touched, Allison felt tears dampen her lashes, but this time she didn't care. "That's so nice of her—and so completely unexpected."

"Can we see Leah and the babies?" Josie asked.

"Sure. The doctor said we could visit in small groups."

Josie, Lara, Allison and Tony, led by Eloise, left the crowded waiting room and walked down the hallway.

"She's in here," Eloise said quietly, and pushed open the door.

Leah was propped up in bed, her newly diminished figure tucked beneath pristine white sheets and blanket. She turned her head as they entered, her smile wide.

"Hello." Her voice was soft, exhaustion evident in her tone, but filled with a quiet elation.

They gathered around her bed.

"Where are the babies?" Josie glanced around the room, eager to see Leah's new family.

"The girls are in the nursery," Leah said. "None of them are over five pounds, and the doctor wants them kept in incubators until they're a bit older. But the nursery is right across the hall and you can see them through the window."

"And how are you doing?" Allison asked, thinking that the new mother fairly glowed.

Leah smiled. "Very well. I was afraid that delivery would be scary since there were three babies instead of one, but it all happened so fast that I didn't have time to be afraid."

Allison thought Leah exuded a kind of radiant peace, and her words reassured her about the future delivery of her own babies as nothing else could have.

"When will you get to go home?" Tony asked.

Allison saw Leah's gaze soften as she looked across the bed at Tony. His very male, muscled body, clothed in dark jacket and jeans, together with his black hair and brown eyes, created a sharp contrast to the females in the room with their colorful clothes and slim figures.

"I'm not sure," Leah replied. "I haven't asked the doctor, but I don't think he'll keep me in hospital very long. The babies will probably remain for a while, however, perhaps until they weigh at least five pounds."

"But they're fine, aren't they? There's nothing wrong?" Allison's voice revealed the quick stab of anxiety that caught at her chest.

"No, nothing's wrong, they're perfectly healthy," Leah hastened to reassure her. "They're perfect but tiny."

"Ah, I see."

"Why don't you all walk across the hall to see them?" Leah urged. "They're beautiful."

"Not that you're prejudiced," Josie teased, her eyes twinkling.

"Not at all," Leah agreed complacently. "But they really are three absolutely perfect babies."

Everyone laughed, they couldn't help it. Leah's pride in her children was unaffected, unshakable and absolute.

"I think we should traipse across the hall and take a look at these superbabies," Tony commented. He winked at Leah and moved to the door, holding it open so the women could file through.

"We'll be right back, Leah," Allison said over her shoulder.

Leah responded with a wave of her hand and a contented smile.

The curtains were open in the long hall window that looked over the nursery area. Only a few feet beyond the clear glass were three little incubators holding tiny little scraps of humanity, a card labeled Simpson slotted at the end of each small bed. Each of the babies were wrapped snugly in a pink blanket with a tiny little knit cap on her head, and the little red faces beneath the pink caps were identical. Two of the babies were sleeping, their eyes closed, lips pursed, but the third was wide-awake, stirring and stretching until finally, as the five adults watched, she opened her mouth and wailed. Seconds later a nurse swept the crying infant into her arms. She glanced up, saw the group at the window and approached to hold the little one up for them to view.

"Oh, isn't she darling?" Allison breathed, fascinated by the tiny, perfectly formed child.

"Yes." Eloise brushed away a tear. "She is."

Tony shifted uncomfortably and patted Eloise awkwardly on the shoulder. "If she's so great, why are you crying?" He nodded at the smiling nurse and red-faced baby on the other side of the glass. "You're making the baby cry."

Eloise laughed. "You may be right, Tony." She waggled her fingers at the baby but was ignored. The nurse met Eloise's gaze, and they both chuckled.

"I suppose we should go back to the waiting room, so someone else can come in and visit." Eloise turned away from the window, and the rest of the group reluctantly followed.

All except Allison. Her gaze followed the nurse as she returned the now-sleeping baby to her incubator. Behind her the voices of her friends greeted Leah, and Allison glanced over her shoulder, the open door allowing her a glimpse of Leah's happy, contented features before the door quietly closed.

She turned back to the nursery and the three beautiful new babies and felt her heart turn over. Her palm instinctively covered the small, barely there bulge of her own babies, and she knew, with sudden fierce certainty, that she had to put aside her insecurity and uncertainties and reach out to Jorge. Her babies, like the amazingly tiny infants in the hospital nursery incubators, deserved the best that life could offer them. They definitely deserved a mother brave enough to fight for their future and her own.

Her mind firmly made up, Allison went back to Leah's room just in time to give her a quick hug before they all returned to the waiting room. The staff of Manhattan Multiples took up nearly every available space in the big room's collection of cushioned sofas and chairs.

"You know what I think?" Lara said as they

queued up to pour coffee into foam cups from the coffee urn atop a small table in a corner of the room.

"No, what?" Allison looked longingly at the coffee urn but chose an herbal teabag and filled her cup from the hot water pot on the tray.

"I think we *have* to find a way to keep Manhattan Multiples' doors open. Seeing Leah with her babies really reinforces the importance of what we do at MM offices."

"I agree." Allison nodded.

"So do I." Eloise's voice joined theirs, and both women turned to see her standing directly behind them. "I only wish I knew how to make it happen."

"Make what happen?" the two people standing behind Eloise inquired, the question loud in an unexpected conversational lull.

The room quieted even further, everyone turning to look expectantly at Eloise.

"Lara and Allison were just saying that we *must* find a way to generate funding for Manhattan Multiples so that we can continue to help new mothers like Leah."

"Hear, hear!" Tony called, lifting his white paper cup.

"The question is," Eloise said, "how are we going to do it?"

"We'll find a way!" someone called from the back.

"Yes. Even if we have to panhandle on the street in front of the offices!"

The group laughed and cheered at the wild suggestion.

"Whatever it takes," Josie said, her mobile features serious, "we'll do. Manhattan Multiples has to stay open. The city needs us."

"She's right. United we stand!"

Eloise's gray eyes filled with tears. "You all are wonderful. Bless you." She lifted her head, chin firming, and nodded decisively. "We'll find a way. We must. Not only does the city need us, but our mothers and their babies need us. We can't let them down."

The group cheered. Allison stayed at the impromptu brainstorming session for ideas to save Manhattan Multiples for another half hour before she said goodbye and headed for home.

Determined to face Jorge with the strength to reach out and grab his offer of a real marriage with both hands, she entered the apartment, hung up her coat and went looking for him.

"Jorge?"

He wasn't in the kitchen or the living room, and she peered into the empty master bedroom before pushing open the door to the soon-to-be nursery that still functioned as Jorge's office.

He was seated at his desk, and he looked over his shoulder when the door opened, his expression both welcoming and wary. He wore comfortable, faded jeans and a cotton shirt, the long sleeves rolled halfway up his forearms. Allison's heart lurched. His hair was rumpled, and he looked good enough to eat.

"Allison. You're home."

"Yes, I am. And we need to resolve some things." She walked toward him.

"I agree. You have to listen to me."

"I don't want to listen to you." She stopped in front of him, so close that she stood between his spread thighs.

"Allison," he began.

He didn't get to finish. Allison grabbed his collar at the same time that she settled on to his lap and covered his mouth with hers. For one terrifying moment he stiffened and went absolutely still. Allison thought she'd done precisely the wrong thing and repulsed him.

But then he wrapped his arms around her and yanked her flush against him, his mouth hot and eager beneath hers, his hands nearly bruising as he cupped the back of her head and held her mouth against his.

She slipped her arms around his neck, shivering with pleasure when his mouth left hers and he buried his face in the hollow of her throat, his lips hot against the pound of her pulse.

"Allison," he muttered, lifting his head to look

down at her. "Thank God." He cupped her bottom and pulled her tighter against him. "You believe me? Because if you don't, I—"

She covered his mouth with her palm, silencing him.

"I believe you," she said, her voice throaty. "And I need to tell you something." She paused, gathered her courage. "I hope you meant it when you told me that you want a real marriage, because that's what I want, too." Relief and heat flared in his eyes, and before he could speak, she hurried on. "But if I ever catch you holding another woman, I swear, Jorge, I'm going to kill you."

His lips quirked, tickling her palm.

"Metaphorically speaking, of course."

His low chuckle escaped her fingers.

She frowned threateningly. "I mean it."

He nodded solemnly, but his eyes laughed at her.

"I'm sorry that I've been so erratic emotionally, but Dr. Kenyan says that even if the mood swings continue all during my pregnancy, there's no reason to expect that I won't be back to my usual calm, stable self after the babies are born."

He rolled his eyes and raised an eyebrow. She frowned at him.

"Dr. Kenyan assured me that I won't continue to have 'boomeranging hormones' after I deliver. But you may have to grit your teeth and bear with me until then."

She drew a deep breath and let it out, frowning at him. He caught her hand in his and looked at her inquiringly. She nodded and he lifted her hand from his mouth, pressed a warm kiss in the palm and looked at her expectantly.

When he didn't speak, Allison narrowed her eyes and glared at him. "What?"

"Aren't you forgetting something?" His voice was raspy, amused, husky with arousal. When she continued to look at him with confusion, he sighed. "Aren't you going to tell me you love me?"

Allison froze, panicking, wondering if he was going to reject her if she was the first to say the words.

He smiled and smoothed his forefinger over the frown lines between her brows. "Because I love you. I think I fell in love with you at first sight, when I looked across that crowded ballroom and saw you."

Allison felt her bones melt, her heart surge with relief. "Oh, Jorge, I love you, too." Tears welled up and overflowed.

His thumb smoothed the salty moisture away from her cheeks. "Honey, you've got to stop crying. And I don't care how erratic you are while you're pregnant, as long as you keep loving me, your hormones can boomerang all they want. I'll be the most patient expectant father in the world."

Allison's eyebrows rose in disbelief, and he burst out laughing.

"Well, I'll try to be the most patient man in the world. How's that?"

"Just as long as you don't stop loving me," she murmured.

"Honey, that's a promise." He stood, covering her mouth with his as he headed for their bedroom. "Just as long as you never stop loving me."

He repeated her words like a vow.

A wedding vow, Allison thought hazily, realizing that all her dreams had come true, just before he stripped off her blouse and she lost herself in her husband's arms.

*   *   *   *   *

Don't miss the stunning conclusion in
Silhouette Special Edition's exciting continuity
MANHATTAN MULTIPLES:
PRINCE OF THE CITY
by Nikki Benjamin
Available November 2003
Don't miss it!

MONTANA MAVERICKS

The Kingsleys

**Nothing is as it seems
beneath the big skies of Montana.**

HER MONTANA MILLIONAIRE
by Crystal Green

(Silhouette Special Edition #1574)

New York socialite Jinni Fairchild was barely surviving Rumor's
slow pace. Until she met Max Cantrell. Tall. Dark. Gorgeous.
And rich as Midas. Would his unhurried sensuality tempt this
fast-lane girl to stop and smell the roses—with him?

Available November 2003 at your favorite retail outlet.

Your opinion is important to us! Please take a few moments to share your thoughts with us about your experiences with Harlequin and Silhouette books. Your comments will be very useful in ensuring that we deliver books you love to read.
Please take a few minutes to complete the questionnaire, then send it to us at the address below.

Send your completed questionnaires to:
Harlequin/Silhouette Reader Survey, P.O. Box 9046, Buffalo, NY 14269-9046

1. As you may know, there are many different lines under the Harlequin and Silhouette brands. Each of the lines is listed below. Please check the box that most represents your reading habit for each line.

Line	Currently read this line	Do not read this line	Not sure if I read this line
Harlequin American Romance	❏	❏	❏
Harlequin Duets	❏	❏	❏
Harlequin Romance	❏	❏	❏
Harlequin Historicals	❏	❏	❏
Harlequin Superromance	❏	❏	❏
Harlequin Intrigue	❏	❏	❏
Harlequin Presents	❏	❏	❏
Harlequin Temptation	❏	❏	❏
Harlequin Blaze	❏	❏	❏
Silhouette Special Edition	❏	❏	❏
Silhouette Romance	❏	❏	❏
Silhouette Intimate Moments	❏	❏	❏
Silhouette Desire	❏	❏	❏

2. Which of the following best describes why you bought *this book?* One answer only, please.

the picture on the cover	❏	the title	❏
the author	❏	the line is one I read often	❏
part of a miniseries	❏	saw an ad in another book	❏
saw an ad in a magazine/newsletter	❏	a friend told me about it	❏
I borrowed/was given this book	❏	other: _____	❏

3. Where did you buy *this book?* One answer only, please.

at Barnes & Noble	❏	at a grocery store	❏
at Waldenbooks	❏	at a drugstore	❏
at Borders	❏	on eHarlequin.com Web site	❏
at another bookstore	❏	from another Web site	❏
at Wal-Mart	❏	Harlequin/Silhouette Reader Service/through the mail	❏
at Target	❏		
at Kmart	❏	used books from anywhere	❏
at another department store or mass merchandiser	❏	I borrowed/was given this book	❏

4. On average, how many Harlequin and Silhouette books do you buy at one time?

I buy _____ books at one time	❏
I rarely buy a book	❏

MRQ403SSE-1A

5. How many times per month do you shop for any *Harlequin and/or Silhouette* books?
   One answer only, please.

1 or more times a week	❑	a few times per year	❑
1 to 3 times per month	❑	less often than once a year	❑
1 to 2 times every 3 months	❑	never	❑

6. When you think of your ideal heroine, which *one* statement describes her the best?
   One answer only, please.

She's a woman who is strong-willed	❑	She's a desirable woman	❑
She's a woman who is needed by others	❑	She's a powerful woman	❑
She's a woman who is taken care of	❑	She's a passionate woman	❑
She's an adventurous woman	❑	She's a sensitive woman	❑

7. The following statements describe types or genres of books that you may be
   interested in reading. Pick *up to 2 types* of books that you are most interested in.

I like to read about truly romantic relationships	❑
I like to read stories that are sexy romances	❑
I like to read romantic comedies	❑
I like to read a romantic mystery/suspense	❑
I like to read about romantic adventures	❑
I like to read romance stories that involve family	❑
I like to read about a romance in times or places that I have never seen	❑
Other: _____	❑

*The following questions help us to group your answers with those readers who are
similar to you. Your answers will remain confidential.*

8. Please record your year of birth below.
   19 _____

9. What is your marital status?

   single ❑   married ❑   common-law ❑   widowed ❑
   divorced/separated ❑

10. Do you have children 18 years of age or younger currently living at home?
    yes ❑   no ❑

11. Which of the following best describes your employment status?

    employed full-time or part-time ❑   homemaker ❑   student ❑
    retired ❑   unemployed ❑

12. Do you have access to the Internet from either home or work?
    yes ❑   no ❑

13. Have you ever visited eHarlequin.com?
    yes ❑   no ❑

14. What state do you live in?

    _____

15. Are you a member of Harlequin/Silhouette Reader Service?
    yes ❑   Account # _____   no ❑   MRQ403SSE-1B

#1573 A LITTLE BIT PREGNANT—Susan Mallery
Readers' Ring
Security expert Zane Rankin could have any woman he wanted…
and often did. Computer hacker and wallflower Nicki Beauman
had contented herself with being platonic with her sexy friend Zane.
Until one night of unbridled—and unexpected—passion changed
their relationship forever….

#1574 HER MONTANA MILLIONAIRE—Crystal Green
Montana Mavericks: The Kingsleys
Sunday driving through life was billionaire and single dad
Max Cantrell's way. Celebrity biographer Jinni Fairchild preferred
living in the fast lane. But when these two opposites collided, there
was nothing but sparks! Could they overcome the detours keeping
them apart?

#1575 PRINCE OF THE CITY—Nikki Benjamin
Manhattan Multiples
When the city's mayor threatened to sever funds for Eloise Vale's
nonprofit organization, she reacted like a mama bear protecting her
cubs. But mayor Bill Harper was her one-time love. Eloise would
fight for Manhattan Multiples, but could she resist the lure of her
sophisticated ex and protect herself from falling for her enemy?

#1576 MAN IN THE MIST—Annette Broadrick
Secret Sisters
Gregory Dumas was searching for a client's long-lost family—
he'd long ago given up looking for love. But in chaste beauty
Fiona MacDonald he found both. Would this wary P.I. give in
to the feelings Fiona evoked? Or run from the heartache he was
certain would follow…?

#1577 THE CHRISTMAS FEAST—Peggy Webb
Dependable had never described Jolie "Kat" Coltrane. But zany and
carefree Kat showed her family she was a responsible adult by
cooking Christmas dinner—with the help of one unlikely holiday
guest. Lancelot Estes, a hardened undercover agent, was charmed
by the artless Kat…and soon the two were cooking up more than
dinner!

#1578 A MOTHER'S REFLECTION—Elissa Ambrose
Drama teacher Rachel Hartwell's latest role would be her most
important yet: befriending her biological daughter. When Rachel
learned that the baby she'd given up for adoption years ago had lost
her adoptive mother, she vowed to become a part of her daughter's
life. But did that include falling in love with Adam Wessler—her
child's adoptive father?